Love-Altared

A Closed-Door Romance Novel

NOELLE DAVENPORT

Copyright

ISBN Print 979-8-9864298-4-7

ISBN eBook 979-8-9864298-3-0

Library of Congress Control Number 2023920504

Cover Art: Cover Ever After

Edits: Black Quill Editing & Lane Luckey

Published by Noelle Davenport in The United States of America

For permissions, please email: noelledauthor@gmail.com

https://www.noelledavenportbooks.com

To those who struggle to love themselves. I see you.
Keep trying.

ONE

Story

There are women in this world who just have their lives together. Their social media posts are filled with lavish vacations and beautiful photographs; their kids and spouses are happy and smiling; their fashion choices, body types, and makeup are flawless. Perfect. Perfect. Perfect. And to tell you the truth, I liked to believe I appeared to be one of these women.

As a youth I strived to be like them, and usually fell flat on my face trying. But now, I had finally made something of myself. I was no longer the "Number Nerd" only welcome in certain circles because my childhood best friend was Mr. Popular. In fact, I left that girl far behind after graduation and never looked back. I'd worked hard to become who I was today.

The hardest part about college for me was not the classes, but in letting go of who I used to be. And eventually, I did. I started wearing my contacts more often, bought a new wardrobe, grew out my hair, and learned how to do more than a "five-minute face" of makeup. Slowly, that girl I left behind in Little Creek was just somebody I used to know. Finally, I was a successful city girl that appeared to be born that way.

On the outside, everything in my life seemed to be going right.

All my ducks were in a row. I wasn't just on my way to having it all, I already did.

Everything revolved around my career, and for the most part, I liked it that way. It was no surprise when my love-life followed suit and my work partner, Dane, and I fell in love. We spent long nights pouring over spreadsheets, spending more time at the office together than we did at our own apartments, so it only made sense when he proposed that I'd say yes. Engaged to a man I could've only ever dreamed of loving a few years ago, he filled any small gaps in my life I couldn't. Life was good. On the outside.

With the wedding right around the corner, I crossed every T and dotted every I, but the stress still pressed down on my shoulders. The whole event dripped with extravagance, which wasn't my original vision. I hesitated spending so much on a wedding in a small, blue-collar farming town. But Dane insisted if we weren't having a big celebration in the city, we needed to bring it with us to the country. He planned a killer honeymoon for us afterward, and honestly, I looked forward more to spending time in the Bahamas than I did to the actual wedding.

All that planning, spending, trying on different dresses, cakes, and foods while working sixty hours a week had taken its toll on me, for sure. I couldn't wait to say I do and leave all the stress behind for a bit.

If I could get through the next few days, everything would be fine. Right?

I had all my emotions stuffed down and in check, until one invite came back, marked "undeliverable." My heart stopped when I saw it in my stack of mail, dredging up feelings I had buried long ago. The envelope was mangled and ripped from the sorting machines, and tape and red stamps covered the front, but I knew whose address was underneath. I caressed what was left of the words my shaky hands wrote on the invite weeks ago when I wondered if I should even send it. Tears welled in my eyes, and my heart ached for the late-night talks, the pinky-promises, and the forevers that would never be. Luke was my best friend, but I

2

convinced myself that part of letting the old Story go meant letting him go too. The guilt of it ate at me for most of my college years, and every time I felt the urge to reignite our bond, I forced myself to let it die. It had been years since I spoke to him face to face, though I never forgot to text him on his birthday, and he on mine. That life was behind me, and worse, he let me leave.

Because of this, something nagged at my soul. A tiny little parasite that wore a raw spot in my completeness. It sat there as an irritant that never fully went away, although I could ignore it quite well most of the time. After all, I had everything I'd ever wanted, right?

But at night, after the hustle slowed down, the makeup was washed off, and I was alone with the vulnerable girl I hid deep within, that piece inside roared like thunder. It swallowed up the silence, enveloped my sense of accomplishment, and made me doubt my worthiness for my achievements. While I didn't want to completely return to the nerdy girl I used to be, I hated how I covered up so much of the parts that made me who I was inside.

I stared at the woman in the mirror and still saw the girl that wanted to fit in. The girl who practiced a song for weeks before the talent show, then froze on stage to the laughter of her peers. The girl who did the cool kids' homework for them just so they'd nod their heads at her as they passed by in the hallway. And I knew that no matter how much makeup I buried her under, or how much money I made, I would always feel like the girl who tried too hard.

I splashed my face with water to erase my thoughts, flipped off the bathroom light, and fell into bed like a zombie.

After a terrible night's sleep debating what to do, I decided to snap a photo of the obliterated envelope and send it to Luke in a text.

> Story: Just wanted you to know that your invite went to hell and back before it was returned to me. I know it's kinda late notice, but you're invited if you want to come. I'm sure Ma's invite is hanging on her fridge, so you'll know when and where. I hope you're well.

I HIT SEND, tossed Luke's invite in the trash, and grabbed my car keys on my way out the door.

My mind wandered throughout my morning commute. *Would Luke even reply? Would he show up at the wedding?* I didn't deserve to hear anything from him after all this time, but my heart still hoped for some kind of contact. I shook the intruding thoughts from my mind and focused out the windshield, searching for signs of spring instead. Not one bud sprouted from the dormant trees that lined the busy streets. Between the skyscrapers and cement jungle, the only evidence that winter was over was the fact the snow had melted and stayed gone.

I parked my Lexus in a spot with my name painted on the cement, then rode the elevator up to the twenty-fifth floor. My ears popped as I neared the top, which was my cue to push down the anxiety wrapping itself around me and put on my "work smile." I grabbed my daily cup of coffee from my assistant's outstretched hand, then headed into the conference room for our morning meeting. I yawned as I nestled into my seat, still trying to shake off the long hours from the day before and opened my laptop.

"Look at you, squeaking in at the last second," my bestie in the city, Olivia, whispered, sliding her chair closer to mine.

"As long as I beat Mr. Wallace, I'm on time," I whispered back.

"Lunch again today? I saw a new food truck I wanted to try."

"I can't. I have a last-minute meeting with the bakery. I'm *so* done with wedding plans at this point. I don't care what kind of frosting they use, I just want it to be over," I said with a tired laugh.

Olivia frowned. "Ladies and gentlemen, Story Madison: the first bride ever who didn't love planning every detail. You're such a weirdo."

"*You* chose to be friends with me, so I guess that makes you a weirdo too."

She squeezed my arm. "I'm going to miss you while you're gone on your honeymoon. Who else can I gossip with on my lunch break while you're gone?"

"Well, you could finally accept an offer from Jason in sales and go out with him."

"Yeah, but he won't care about girl talk," she whined.

"It's only ten days. Then we'll have tons of stuff to talk about when I get back."

She grinned. "Fine. But only if you bring me back something pretty from the Bahamas."

"Deal," I said, shaking her hand.

Dane sat down across from me, and I found it deeply unfair that he worked the same hours I did, yet he looked bright-eyed and bushy tailed. All the while I'd struggled to cover up the dark circles under my eyes this morning. I had to throw my hair into a messy bun, because I didn't have time to wash it—again. Some guys have all the luck, I guess.

Halfway through the meeting I zoned out and drifted off to my apartment where my precisely made bed was waiting for me. I wondered how many hours I would be putting in today, and if my pillow missed me the way I missed it.

"Astoria?" My boss's voice broke through my sleepy daydream as Olivia elbowed me.

"Yes?" I replied, straightening in my chair.

"What is the status on the Hansen Foods account? Are you and Dane set to blow last month's numbers out of the water again?"

I flipped open my notebook and glanced at my notes. "I spoke to Hansen Foods' rep yesterday, and although their contract with us is set to expire next quarter, he's confident they will re-sign with me. Er, I mean, us."

"Splendid. That's my Dream Team! All of you take note: Dane and Astoria are shining examples on how to make me money." He turned his attention to me. "The Hansen account is your baby, and we wouldn't have snagged them without you. Those farmers sure love a small-town, farm girl. If we can get them to sign a new contract, there will be a nice little bonus in it for you and Dane," Mr. Wallace said, taking off his reading glasses and shutting his laptop. "That is all for today."

I made my way back to my office and hung my cardigan on the hook next to the door. Dane slipped in behind me, nudging the door shut, and moved a stray hair away from my neck to plant a kiss.

"I know we aren't supposed to do any PDA at work, but I can't help it when you have your hair all pulled up like this," he whispered into my neck.

Goosebumps rushed down my arms.

"I mean, don't get me wrong. Dark, cascading curls hanging down your back are nice too, but I'm sorta digging this sexy accountant vibe you've got going on today."

"Let me guess, all I need to complete the look is a pair of glasses?"

He grinned. "Absolutely. Can I stick around long enough for you to put on your blue-light-filtering ones?"

I turned to face him and smacked his arm playfully. "You are nothing but trouble," I said, giggling.

"I'll take that as a compliment," he said with a wry grin and kissed my lips.

I leaned my back against the closed door. "That's up for interpretation."

"How many more days until our wedding?" he asked, moving closer.

"Ten days. Finally."

"It can't come soon enough, future Mrs. Michaels."

He pinned me between his muscular arms, and I gladly surrendered ground.

How he had time to work like he did and still hit the gym baffled me, I could barely drag myself out of bed lately. I thought growing up on a farm was hard, but life moved so much faster here in the city, I never had time to rest.

I smiled and ran my fingers through his surfer-blond hair before planting a kiss on his forehead. "I completely agree. But in the meantime, we've both got work to do so we can actually *relax* on the beach, instead of working the entire time."

"*Fiiiiine.*" He dropped his hands to the doorknob. "You win this time, but keep in mind, if you walk past my office looking like that all day long, I'm not going to be able to concentrate on anything else."

"I'm looking forward to being your distraction." I pushed him playfully into the hallway. "Now get to work. The world is waiting to give us their money."

"Yes, ma'am," he replied, mocking the boys back home. "Isn't that how the farm boys say it?"

"Not with that Chicago accent, they don't." I laughed and watched as he walked away.

See? I told you I had it all. Life was perfect.

Until ... it wasn't.

TWO

Story

The bridal room bustled with chattering women getting ready for my big day. The fog of perfume and aerosol hairspray settled around curling irons and lipstick tubes, suffocating me just as much as my restless thoughts. The door burst open, revealing a flushed and very late bridesmaid.

"I'm so sorry I'm late, Stor, I couldn't find my Booze Bag," she panted.

I paused from putting on my mascara. "Your what?"

"You know, my Booze Bag. The one I bring to all special occasions. Weddings, graduations ... baby showers," she muttered the last one under her breath. "The one with tons of pockets inside that I can hide those tiny bottles of booze in?"

"Ah. *That* Booze Bag," I said, shaking my head. "The one you brought to girls' night out ... at a bar?"

If it were anyone else besides Liz, I'd be upset that she was late. But she'd been late to everything since the day she was born, so I had come to terms with it. I loved her hot mess, and she loved mine.

"Yeah. That's the one," she said, diving through the bottom of her dress and pulling it down over her body. "Now, someone come help me get zipped!" She backed up into the nearest bridesmaid. "There's a tiny bottle of Captain Morgan with your name on it if you help this girl glam up."

And with that, a swarm of blush-colored satin dresses circled her, leaving me alone for five seconds to breathe.

Above the din, Liz yelled, "Hey, Stor, can you hand me one of the tiny peach vodkas in the inside pocket?"

I set down my makeup brush and crossed the room. My hand dove to the bottom of a bag that only an alcoholic Mary Poppins would carry, and grabbed at who-knows-what in the bottom.

Crumpled and smashed beneath several tiny bottles was a yellow envelope with my name on it, written in Luke's handwriting. I slipped my finger under the open flap and unfolded the paper inside. My stomach dropped when I saw that the date scrawled across the top was from the night before I left for college. Why would Liz have a letter written to me from Luke from so long ago? I tucked it under my elbow, passed the bottle to Liz's hand appearing above the swarm, and stepped out onto the balcony to read in peace.

> *Dear Story,*
> *You're my best friend in the whole world, and I have told you every deep, dark secret I've ever had, except one:*
> *I'm in love with you.*
> *I have been since the third grade. I've loved you through awkward growth spurts and braces. I have loved you through our movie nights in, prom dates, and graduation. And I love you now, even though you're leaving. I can't seem to get used to the idea of letting you go.*
> *I can't live any more of my life without you. I want you to be mine forever, and although I'm terrified to tell you, I can't risk losing you. I want to spend every day after this laughing and crying through life with you by my side.*
> *Remember that night we talked about being old people rocking on our porch while the grandkids play on the lawn? Well, that gave me something to work toward. When I*

*wanted to give up and let go of the dream of you and me, I
pictured you with gray hair and smile lines around your beautiful eyes from years of laughter, and it has kept me going. You
keep me going. And I don't want to live another day without
leaning up against you. Let's build a good life together. Don't
go. Stay.*

    I love you, Story.

    Love, Luke

The wind ripped from my lungs as I read the letter over and
over again. The balcony tipped sideways, and I sat abruptly in a
cold metal chair to keep from toppling over. I clutched the paper
between my shaking hands and blinked as tears left their marks on
my white silk robe.

"Why didn't he ever tell me?" I whispered to myself.

Liz stepped out onto the balcony and yelled, "The party can
start now! I'm single and ready to—" but stopped short when she
saw the letter.

"Oh, boy ..." She fidgeted with her dress and sat in the other
chair beside me.

"'Oh, boy?' That's all you have to say about this?" I shook the
letter at Liz. "Why do you have this? And why didn't you
tell me?"

Liz's shoulders fell. "I found it on the ground at your going
away party under Luke's chair. I held on to it for you, because you
were moving on with your life and getting the hell out of Little
Creek. Then the longer I kept it, the more I struggled with the
idea of giving it to you. Eventually, I threw my bag under my bed
with the letter inside, and I forgot all about it. I'm sorry. I thought
if you knew Luke loved you too, that you'd throw away your plans
for college and stay home. Luke had no right to mess that up for
you."

"But you aren't the one who got to decide that for me," I said,
wiping my cheeks.

"Stor—"

"Don't 'Stor' me! You knew! And you didn't tell me!"

"Although Luke was All-American everything in high school, he is quicksand now, Story. Staying here to be with him would've sucked the life out of you, and I couldn't bear to see you lose everything you worked so hard for. Chicago and Dane have been so good for you! It was the right choice to leave Little Creek behind. You finally got your ticket out of this hole, and you have completely changed everything about yourself."

That nag inside me dusted off its boots and started line-dancing on my heart. And not a cute, Cowboy Cha-Cha. But the loudest, clappiest, stompiest line dance that ever existed. In fact, I was pretty sure it made up a new one, just for me. *Yay.*

"I'm not so sure that changing everything about myself in order to fit in was what I needed," I said quietly through my tears.

"Seriously, Stor?" Liz said with a laugh. "Your amazing life in Chicago is far more adventurous than anything Little Creek has to offer you. Don't you remember high school? Believe me, you want the city life you have."

My mind was swept back to the lonely nights in my apartment when the walls seemed to close in around me, and the ache for quiet, wide-open spaces returned.

"I know it looks fantastic, but it's not all it's cracked up to be sometimes."

"If you were miserable there, why didn't you come home?"

"It's not that I was miserable, per se, but I knew I couldn't come back and fit into that box everyone put me in growing up. And I didn't want to be labeled a failure or a quitter. I was finally standing confidently on my own, and once I saw what I could be without everyone telling me who I was, I ran with it. I kept forcing myself to stay because I was successful at college, and then on fire at my job. I am happy ... most of the time, anyway. But marrying Dane cements my choice to stay in Chicago forever. I've traded the sounds of cicadas and frogs at night, for traffic and sirens in a city that never sleeps. I just never realized how much I missed it until I came back."

"You're choosing a life with a very successful man," Liz argued. "He can give you a life most of us can only dream of, Stor. You aren't changing your mind, are you?"

"I don't know, I wish I had more time to process this. I need a minute alone to think."

"Well, think quick. You have a wedding starting soon." Liz stood and slipped back through the sliding door. Before she closed it, she said over her shoulder, "Dane is good for you, Stor. Don't throw that away. Take the chance to get out of here for those of us who will never get one."

The roar of an old truck engine grew louder from below, and I immediately knew that sound. It rumbled in sync with my heartbeat and awoke a million memories within me. I stood and looked over the balcony as Luke pulled into the parking lot. He opened the creaky door, slammed it shut, and threw a blazer on as he walked toward the church steps. He looked so handsome in his "good jeans" without wear marks or holes in them and a suit coat I'd never seen before. His broad shoulders held the burdens of an overworked, under-appreciated farmer well; and the way his muscular body walked with purpose hit me like a sledgehammer.

He was average height for a man around here, which is probably the only reason he didn't get football scholarship offers from every college in the Midwest. But he carried himself with confidence, and I'd always looked up to him—literally and metaphorically.

He paused beside a long Buick with an old lady standing next to it, and then turned and ran back to his truck. He returned with a jack in one hand and a star wrench in the other. He handed the old lady his blazer and proceeded to change her flat tire in the gravel parking lot.

She pinched his cheeks and squished his face before hugging him tightly with gratitude. He tossed the tools back in the bed of his truck and wiped his hands on a bandana he carried in his pocket. He dusted off his now-dirty jeans, and put his suit coat back on before escorting his new friend into the church.

I smiled through tear-filled eyes as I watched the most selfless person I'd ever met put someone else first. On a day when he had every excuse to be heartbroken, selfish, and angry, he looked outward and helped his fellow man.

My mind churned with questions I needed answered. Did his heart ache? Was he over me? That letter was written years ago. Did he even care anymore?

"Stor, your mom's back to help you get into your dress," Liz said from the doorway. "Just forget this whole thing and let your dreams come true. You've got a great guy waiting for you downstairs."

"Yeah, I know," I said with a sigh and stood, folding the letter and sliding it back into the envelope. "But how can he love me for who I am when he hasn't seen every part of me?" I whispered to myself.

Although my body was occupied with finishing touches on makeup and hair, my mind raced. I had always loved Luke. He was my best friend in the world, and he knew all my secrets. He was kind and genuine, and when it wasn't cool to be friends with a nerdy girl, he made it cool. Everyone sort of accepted me on the outskirts of the popular crowd because Luke and I were a package deal. Without him, I would've been eaten alive by those kids, I'm sure of it.

Luke Dixon was an old soul, steady and hard-working, and always had been. He loved others. And he *maybe* still loved me. Should I rethink things before I promised to love, honor, and cherish another man? Could I, in good conscience, make that promise knowing I had unfinished business with Luke? Would I always wonder what if?

"Boy, you are one bummed-out-looking bride," a familiar voice said over my shoulder.

I glanced up into the mirror to see my mother in the reflection behind me. The vanity lights highlighted the tears welling in my eyes, so I did my best to force a smile.

"Just deep in thought," I said, stepping numbly into my dress.

"What are you thinking about, dead puppies?" Mama asked as she zipped.

I laughed through my tears. "No, but I need to ask you something. Do you think I've changed too much of who I am?"

Mama laughed. "Where is this coming from, baby girl?"

"I've just been having a lot of nagging thoughts lately about if Dane really loves *me* or just his idea of me. I've been so good at hiding the girl I used to be to be accepted, that I'm not sure he knows every part of who I am. I've kept my highlights front and center and my bloopers hidden for so long. What if he marries me and is disappointed with behind-the-curtain Story?"

"Well, you *have* changed yourself a lot since you left home. But that doesn't mean you are less loveable. I thought you were happy with who you've become. Are you not?"

"Mostly. But I feel like I haven't been honest with Dane, *or* myself for that matter. Any time I let out pieces of the old me, he seems put-off by it."

"You'll never fully lose everything about yourself, baby. And you ought to be proud of who you were, *and* who you've become. If you're not, you may want to ask yourself why that is."

Mama's words hit me hard. Was I ashamed of myself? And if so, why?

I sighed as Mama clasped Grandma's pearls around my neck. "Before this wedding starts, I need to do something. Have you seen Luke?"

"Last I saw he was being smothered by an old lady, and then he ducked outside into the courtyard."

"Perfect. Thank you." I picked up the hem of my dress, ran out of the bride's room, and raced down the stairway.

I rounded the corner and found Luke pacing, his shoulders slumped and defeated. My heart ripped slowly along a scar I thought had long-since healed as I studied him from the dark hallway. I took off my heels and tiptoed toward him. My thoughts immediately ran off to a life where *he* was the one standing in front of the preacher. And I was walking toward him down the aisle—instead of through a dimly-lit courtyard.

I tapped him on the shoulder, and he whipped around.

"Hey, what are you doin' out here?" His trembling voice betrayed his tough exterior.

"I need to talk to you about something," I whispered as I pulled his letter from behind my back.

His eyes grew wide, and his mouth slacked open. "Where did you get that?" he asked as he lunged for the letter.

I dodged just enough to keep it from him. "That's not important right now. I don't have a lot of time and I need to clarify some things."

Luke ran a shaking hand through his dark hair and straightened his posture. "That was a long time ago, Story."

"I know. But did you mean it?"

"Of course I did."

"Then why didn't you say anything? After all these years, you kept this from me. I thought we were more to each other than that."

"I thought we were too. Then you ran off to college and disappeared from my life. You've barely called me or messaged me in eight years, Stor. It didn't feel fittin' to barge into your life and drop a bomb on you like that."

Luke sighed heavily and sat on a bench. I followed his lead and rested my hand on his knee like I'd done a million times. But this time it felt different.

"Even after all that time with you gone, I wanted to. I planned to tell you that weekend you came home for your parents' anniversary party, and you had a fiancé on your arm. I wanted to tell you every day you were gone. And every day, I chickened out. I had so many unsent texts, so many crumpled-up letters, so many calls I hung up before you answered. Remember that time I drove to the university? I was gonna tell you then, but you looked like you were doin' so much better without me, I couldn't do it. And when you announced your engagement, I wanted to tell you more than anything," he said quietly, rubbing the back of his neck. "But you were so happy. And I didn't want to ruin that for you. I couldn't lose what little of you I had left," he said, his hazel eyes blinking back tears.

"So, you took off," I said flatly. "I wondered why you ducked out so early that night."

"Yeah, well, I was watchin' the girl of my dreams slip through my fingers like sand. I couldn't stomach it in front of a crowd."

"Liz found this at my going-away party." I stroked the weathered edges of the envelope. "She kept it a secret from me. I found it in her purse upstairs."

"That's some bad timin' if I ever saw it," he replied, forcing a laugh. "I'm sorry. I don't want to ruin your big day. I know you love Dane, Story. I'm not about to get in the way of that, no matter how I feel. Let's just call it water under the bridge and move on."

My heart pounded. I could barely focus, and my stomach twisted in knots. As hard as it would be to hear the answer to this question that screamed in my brain, I had to ask him. I swallowed hard, and before I lost the courage I blurted out, "Do you still love me, Luke?"

The color drained from his face, and he cleared his throat again like he always did when he was nervous. "I'm not sure how to answer that, Stor."

"The truth will do just fine."

"What should I do? Lie and say no and watch you marry a guy who doesn't deserve you? Or ruin your weddin' day and say yes? You've been my best friend my whole life—of course I love you. How could I not? Look at you. You're the most incredible woman I've ever met. You are the only person who has ever made me feel important just the way I am. You give me purpose and joy, and when you smile, time goes slower and faster, all at once."

An involuntary smile stretched across my face, making the tear-filled banks of my eyes spill over.

"Yep, just like that." He smiled back and wiped my cheek

with his calloused thumb. "And that's not even the most beautiful thing about you. Your heart is what got me all tangled up inside when I was a lonely, eight-year-old new kid sittin' on a swing all by myself. You were my friend when I had nobody." He exhaled sharply and his tone hardened, "But that ship has sailed, Story. We both know you're marryin' someone else today. He's everything I'm not, and he can give you everything I can't: a fancy penthouse in the city, a nice life full of ritzy parties and late nights out on the town. You deserve that. You deserve a skyline filled with city lights and more than three stations on your radio. And that's somethin' I've been tryin' to come to terms with. If I can't be the one who makes you happy, I'm glad you found a lucky guy who can."

"But—" I argued.

He put his hand up to silence me. "If you hadn't found that letter today, would you even be doubtin' your decision right now?"

"It's more complicated than that, Luke."

"No, it isn't, Stor. Go through with your plans and live the life of your dreams. Don't let me spoil that for you. This is already hard enough," his voice shook.

"Luke …"

"Stop. Don't throw away an amazin' life for me. Only a fool folds a winnin' hand. I can't give you anythin' but hard work on a couple acres and the struggle to make ends meet. Dane can give you a real nice life. Take it."

My chin trembled and my tears spattered the front of my dress.

"Don't cry," he begged as he shook the dusty bandana from his jacket pocket to dab my face. "Sorry, this is all I have," he said with a weak smile.

"I wish I had more time to think about this," I whispered.

"I'm glad you don't. I don't want to be the one who keeps you from your dream life, Stor. You'd resent me eventually and I'd never be able to live with that. Now go, 'cause I'm gonna need a minute to compose myself before I have to watch your daddy give you away." He stood and pulled me to my feet.

I wrapped my arms around his torso, and he pulled me in tight. He buried his face in my hair and kissed the top of my head —breaking my heart in one fell swoop—then pushed me to arm's length.

He looked me in the eyes and his tone was soft, yet sharp on the edges, "No more cryin', you hear? This is the happiest day of your life, remember?" He forced a smile. "Now git before the groom sees you. It's bad luck," he said so quietly it sounded painful.

My feet got heavier with every step I took away from him. My broken heart pounded in my chest and the lump in my throat strangled my ability to breathe.

"Hey, Stor?" he called after me.

I turned and looked over my shoulder. His face twisted as he struggled to keep his composure. He never was good at hiding his feelings from me. Yet maybe he was. He hid this from me for all those years.

"You're the most beautiful bride I have ever seen." He forced a smile and wiped his eyes.

"Thanks, Lukie." I sobbed and disappeared through the doorway.

THREE

Story

My knees shook as I stood with my dad in the foyer as each member of the wedding party stepped through the doorway into the chapel. Thanks to the rum and Dr. Pepper Liz mixed up for me, I had managed to stop crying long enough to touch up my makeup and pull myself together. But my palms began to sweat, and my heart pounded in my ears, so I didn't even hear when the organ struck up *Here Comes the Bride*.

"That's our cue," my dad whispered, wrapping my arm around his.

I painted on a smile and stepped through the doorway to face my uncertain future. Dane stood stiffly at the end of the aisle, with the same painted-on smile. I took a deep breath and began the mile-long walk to a man I was no longer one hundred percent sure about. My throat tightened around the air I forced in and out, threatening to release the floodgates at any moment.

Luke stood alone in the back of the chapel, tears streaming down his face, holding his heart in his hands. When I caught a glimpse of him, a rush of butterflies filled me. In my heart of hearts, I knew in that moment Luke was the man I wished I was vowing to love forever. No matter how far away I'd move, or how high up my penthouse, my heart belonged in the middle of the country, with a humble man who worked from sunup to sundown.

My dad's hug at the end of the aisle was all that was holding me steady as my body wavered and I clung to him to delay the inevitable.

Dane took my hand and smiled, but tension hijacked his face. His clammy hands held mine and the pastor began—not that I was able to focus on anything being said. But when the pastor uttered the famous words, "Does anyone have a reason why these two should not be joined?" my nerves surged.

It's now or never Story.

I looked desperately around the room, wishing Luke would object, only to find his seat empty. I panicked and a sob caught in my throat. I cleared it away to make way for the words I knew I needed to say, but struggled to come up with. I opened my mouth to object before it was too late. My mind raced as everything played in slow motion, but before I could speak, movement out of the corner of my eye drew my attention toward the back of the chapel. Dane's face froze, and he locked eyes with the mystery woman who stood up among a sea of the seated.

"I do," the woman squeaked, cleared her throat, then repeated, "I do. I object."

Dane dropped my hand and looked from the mystery woman, to the pastor, then to me.

"Well," Pastor Federicks laughed uncomfortably, "I've never actually had this happen before. Let's take a short break to figure this out." He shut his bible and removed his reading glasses.

I gripped my bouquet, strangling the flowers in my hand. My breath filled my lungs and then refused to leave. Heat rose in my cheeks with embarrassment, as hundreds of eyes bored holes into me. As if standing under a bright spotlight, sweating with stage fright, I couldn't see more than a few feet in front of me. I was reliving my humiliating junior high talent show performance all over again. Yet the strangest sensation followed: relief. It rested on my shoulders as I glanced between Dane and the woman in the back. I wanted to punch her and hug her all at the same time.

"Who is that woman, Dane?"

"Uh," he coughed, "that is my ex-fiancée, Daphne. She, um, broke off our engagement right before you and I met. Believe me, I'm just as surprised to see her here as you are."

"Oh, I'm not so sure about that." I scoffed.

"I need a minute," Dane whispered.

"Yeah. I know exactly what you mean," I replied, and a crowd of family and bridesmaids circled me.

Dane rushed down the aisle and out the chapel doors with Daphne. Hushed whispers followed them like the wave at a ball game as they passed by. As much as I didn't want to hear what she had to say, I had to know. I pushed my way through the growing crowd, following Dane's path toward the exit and peered through a gap in the big wooden doors.

"Daphne, what are you doing here?"

"I couldn't let you do it, Dane. I've regretted letting you go since the moment I left you. And when I found out you were getting married, I had to make sure you still didn't have feelings for me, like I still have for you."

Dane shoved his hands into his pockets and kicked the gravel under his feet. "Well, I mean, yeah. I do. But you ended things, so I tried to move on. Astoria is an amazing woman ..."

"I'm sure she is—"

"But she's not you," he interrupted.

"So, what are you saying?" Daphne asked, taking his hand.

"I'm saying I still love you too. And I won't go through with this if you'll give us another chance."

"I was hoping you would say that." She squealed like a spoiled brat who got her way and wrapped her arms around him.

I stood frozen in the doorway, fighting for air. As much as I was hoping something would stop the wedding, it still stung like a swarm of angry hornets when I got my wish. My eyes burned with familiar tears as I stepped through the door. I cleared my throat to make my presence known.

"Astoria, I can explain," Dane groveled, pushing Daphne backward slightly.

"No need. This is a bullet I'm glad I dodged," I said, walking toward them. I shoved my bouquet into his chest. "Have a nice life, Dane," I choked out and pivoted on my heels, slamming the heavy wooden church doors behind me.

The darkness in the foyer enveloped me as I crumpled to the floor and wept. But nobody else knew I was more grateful than sad. All I needed right then was to cry. So, I did.

I bawled until my face was splotchy and swollen. I cried while I hung my wedding dress back on its hanger. I cried while my mom unpinned my hair and put my veil away. I cried when I got into the back seat of my parents' car—instead of climbing into the passenger seat of Dane's car with *Just Married* written on the back. I cried out every emotion that tumbled inside until I was pretty sure I was all dried up.

The rest of the night was a blur. I sat numbly on my parents' porch swing and stared out into the dark starlit sky. My breaths sounded foreign in my ears, and the only familiar thing I could grab onto was that particular squeak in the swing's chain. I rocked slowly, without purpose, back and forth, almost like an out-of-body experience.

Liz's voice broke through my brain fog, "How are you doing, Stor?" She climbed the creaky wood steps to the swing I slouched on and rested her hand on my knee as she sat down.

"Well, I've had better days," I tried to joke.

"Is there anything I can do?"

"I have two tickets to Nassau in my bag, and I'm already packed. I think I'll go on my honeymoon and do some soul-searching. Come with me?" I whimpered.

"I wish I could, but I start my new job on Monday," Liz said, frowning. "But you should go. It'll be good for you."

"You know what?" I said as I got an idea. "I think you're right."

FOUR

Luke

Word spread fast through town that Story got left at the altar. My heart ached for her and what she must be feeling, but was it wrong that I was also ecstatic? I mean, I came about as close to losing the girl of my dreams as a man could, and I was still given a second chance. The question was, what on Earth was I gonna do about it?

I paced the hallway in my creaky farmhouse enough times I'd memorized which floorboards I needed to fix. Then my phone chimed.

> Story: Hey, Lukie, I need someone to talk to, and my mom keeps trying to feed me. You up for a drive?

I JUMPED at the chance to see her on a day when I thought she wouldn't want to see anybody. I grabbed my keys with shaky hands and hopped into my truck. The engine was rumbling before I replied.

Luke: Be there in 5.

WHEN I PULLED INTO HER FOLKS' driveway, she sat slumped on the porch steps. Her red eyes and splotchy face told me she'd been crying all day long and it made my chest hurt. If I ever get a hold of that jerk, I'd knock him out for hurting her, then buy him a beer for giving me another shot.

"Hey," I said gently, as I hopped out of the truck and opened the passenger door for her.

She stayed where she was, so I walked up the sidewalk and sat down beside her. "Crazy day, huh?"

"You missed all the action," her voice scratched, raw in her throat.

"Yeah. Sorry 'bout leavin' early. I couldn't stand to watch you give your golden heart to a man I didn't think deserved it."

She laughed. But not a happy laugh. More like an ironic, I-can't-believe-this-happened-to-me laugh. I wrapped my arm around her and pulled her to my shoulder like I had a hundred times in our life.

"I know how embarrassed you must feel, bein' that this is pretty much your worst nightmare come true."

She started to cry again, and I wiped her cheek with my hand-kerchief.

Before she left, I had been the only one who understood her without words. I was the one she told her deepest, darkest secrets to. She trusted me with the insecurities she stuffed deep down. But one question weighed heavily on my mind: did she still?

When she confessed to me that she wanted to give up the pretenses of being a straight-A student, how she secretly hated that she was voted, "Most Likely to Succeed," and that she wanted to rebel and throw it all away; I was the one who convinced her to keep trying. Not because that was what everyone told her to do, but because she was so smart, she ought to earn a good life for herself. So, I guess it was partly my fault when she took my advice to conquer the world and left me staring at her tail lights.

I'd never forget the day she left me behind. Her dream was to move away from Little Creek and start fresh, and mine was to stay there forever. That was why I didn't beg her to stay. Why I didn't sprint down that dusty road after her car like I wanted to. And that was why I chickened out every time I wanted to tell her I loved her. Because she deserved more than I could give her, and she always had.

The front door opened and Penny, Story's mama, peeked her head out. "Oh, good, Luke's here, Paul," she said over her shoulder into the house. "I was just coming out to see if you were hungry, baby girl."

"Nah. I'm good, Mama. Luke and I are going to go for a drive. Don't wait up," she said as she stood from the steps.

Her mama nodded at me and smiled. "I always know she's in good hands when she's with you, Luke. You be safe now."

Story wrapped her arm around my elbow, and I steadied her pace as we walked down the sidewalk. I opened my truck door, and she climbed in and scooted across the bench seat. As I slammed her door shut, I flashed back to the last time I had helped her into my truck.

Eight years earlier

MY TRUCK BOUNCES DOWN *the road through the dark country night, and I feel the clutch slip a bit as I shift. Man, I need to take the time to look at that.*

Story sings loudly to the radio in the passenger seat. The volume she chooses is directly proportional to the headache she'll wake up with tomorrow morning. Still, even three sheets to the wind, she makes me smile. And I'm glad I'm the one she depends on to rescue her from too many shots of tequila.

"Hey, Stor, we're comin' up on your parents' street. Do you want me to take you home?" I holler over the music as I turn the dial down.

"You're such a buzzkill," she slurs as she reaches for the radio knob but misses. "I don't want my mom to see me looking all run over, so can I sleep with you?"

Wait. What? I shake my head to unscramble her words into what she really means. "Of course. Ma's guest room is always open for you, you know that. I'll let your mama know so she doesn't worry."

"That's why I love you. You're so good to me; my bestest pal ever."

She pats my hand on the gear shift, and I hate that even when she's several drinks deep, she still shoves me in the friend zone.

Everything tilts when she asks me the question I don't exactly know how to answer, "Lukie, do you love me too?"

Now, in my super-sober, logical brain, I know that not only does she not realize the depth of what she's asking, but also that there's no way she'll remember my answer in the morning. So, I call my shot and swing for the fence. "Story," I say, gripping the steering wheel, "I have been in love with you since the third grade." I muster every ounce of courage I have and look over at her.

What I see in her eyes makes me panic. For a flash of a second, I see clarity.

She blinks several times and I'm not sure if she's gonna tear up or laugh in my face. She chooses door number three and pukes all over the floorboards instead.

Lovely. Just the reaction a guy wants when he confesses his life-long feelings for the girl he's always loved.

I pull over, grab the hair tie she keeps on my gear shift, and tie her hair out of her face while she defiles my truck. For a few seconds, I wonder if this old beast can be hosed out, or if the smell of puke will forever haunt me about this night.

She grabs my faded bandana from the rearview and wipes her face before she bursts into tears and apologizes profusely. Her first

27

and probably last time getting sloshed, it figures she'd be an emotional drunk.

By the time I get home and finish kinda cleaning up the mess, she's snoring against the passenger window.

I scoop her into my arms and kick the door shut with my boot. Then again, maybe I should leave it open to air out overnight. *I clomp up the porch, realizing even as petite as Story is, dead-weight is dead-weight. I'm embarrassed that this farm boy struggles a bit as she dangles in my arms like a Raggedy-Ann doll. This isn't exactly how I imagined I'd carry her across the threshold, but hey, beggars can't be choosers, right? I relish the moment anyway.*

I head down the hallway toward the square of moonlight in the doorway of the guest room and set her down softly on the comforter. I peel off her boots before tucking her in under a blanket Ma made.

I debate whether I should remove her vomit-splashed jeans but decide against it. I can always wash the blankets, but there's no way I can take her pants off and feel good about it.

I stand up and laugh at the mess she is. Even at her worst she has my heart. I love and hate it at the same time.

I go to the kitchen, grab a glass of water and two aspirin, and leave them on the nightstand. Then I pull the curtains tight and flip off the lamp. She'll feel this one tomorrow morning, and she's got a long drive ahead of her.

I sit in the overstuffed chair next to the bed and watch her sleep. I can't ignore that the game clock has almost run out for her and me, so I allow myself to hurt inside for the sake of it all. The pain of letting her go tomorrow surrounds me and pulls me into despair— just for a moment. Tomorrow I'll be strong for her, but tonight, while no one is watching, I'll cry.

FIVE

Story

"I still don't know how you talked me into this," Luke mumbled as he juggled his passport and carry-on. "I haven't seen the ocean in almost twenty years, Stor. Now here I am, about to go on your honeymoon with ya."

"Did I tell you again how grateful I am that you're coming with me?" I blinked my pathetically swollen eyes at him. "You're the best ever."

"Yeah, well. Goin' on another man's honeymoon feels weird, that's all."

"You forget, he chose someone else—"

"Which he's a complete idiot for," Luke said, shaking his head. "I just always imagined things ... differently ..." he trailed off.

It warmed my heart that I had Luke looking out for me. But deep down, I wasn't quite sure how to approach the elephant in the room between us. I figured if I could persuade him to go to Nassau with me, we'd have plenty of time to talk things out away from the prying eyes of our small town. Fingers crossed for luck that we could figure this whole mess out without ruining our friendship.

Checking in at the airport went seamlessly and the line at

security looked pretty short compared to some flights I'd taken. But that was the *only* perk of being here at three o'clock in the morning. I clutched my travel pillow in one hand and my cold coffee in the other as we shuffled toward security. I was grateful that the farm boy I brought along was a morning person, because I most certainly was not anymore.

As we rounded the corner toward the line, a familiar voice interrupted my train of thought, "You can't be serious right now," Dane huffed. "Where do you think you're going, Astoria?"

My resolve weakened. Dane had kicked my heart in all its freshly bruised places, and apparently came back for round two.

But Luke's simple gesture of his hand on my back gave me the courage to face Dane.

"I'm going on our honeymoon, Dane. Where do you think I'm going?"

"Who is this bozo?" Dane demanded, nodding at Luke.

Daphne giggled behind him.

My urge to punch her took the lead over my urge to hug her from yesterday.

I felt Luke's fingers stiffen on my back and I knew I'd have to get rid of them quickly or we'd all be escorted out by security.

"This is the guy who's taking your plane ticket," I said, squaring my shoulders. "Luke has been my best friend since we were kids, and he's gracious enough to come with me to Nassau so I don't have to be alone on our honeymoon."

Daphne pouted and whimpered, tugging on Dane's arm. "Uh, I was actually bringing Daphne along, so *we* could use the tickets. She thought Nassau would be a great place for us to start fresh," Dane insisted.

"Well, the early bird catches the worm, Dane. Me and Luke have been here for over an hour and your ticket has already been changed into his name. Sorry. You two will have to 'start fresh' somewhere else."

"You can't do that, Astoria! Those tickets were a gift from the firm!"

"Well, I'll be sure to give them a nice thank you note, then. Better yet, maybe I'll send a postcard. Oh, look, the line is moving. Gotta go!" I said over my shoulder and grabbed Luke's arm.

I dragged him away as fast as I could from Dane and through the security checkpoint. I could feel Dane's eyes burning into the back of my head and imagined the fit Daphne was throwing as we collected our carry-ons from the conveyor belt. I never once looked back. I'm not gonna lie, it felt amazing.

SIX

Luke

Fifth Grade

"Story, where are you takin' me?" I hiss through the darkness as she drags me through the cornfield.

"Just wait, it's super cool, Luke," she replies over her shoulder, pushing up her glasses.

Her hair blows into her face as she runs, holding my arm, and for the first time in our friendship, I notice how pretty she's getting. Her teeth are all grown in now, and they don't look too big for her face like they did a few years ago. She's almost as tall as I am and stronger than she looks. I can still whoop her in a game of trampoline wrestling, but it's getting harder than it used to be.

"How much further, Stor? Ma and Pa Dixon don't know I left after supper, and I'll be in big trouble if they find out I'm not in the barn."

She stops abruptly and I run into her, knocking her forward. "We're here," she says, trying to catch her breath

She shines her flashlight a few yards in front of us at a burrow in the dry grass, and eight sets of glowing eyes peer back at us.

"I found an opossum nest when I was exploring earlier, and Liz *wouldn't come see it with me in the dark," she whispers. "She just laughed when I told her what I found."*

"Why'd you ask Liz first? What am I, chopped liver?"

"Of course not, silly. You're my best friend. But you're a boy. Liz is one of my only girl-friends. But I should've known she'd say no. I'll save all the adventurous stuff for you from here on out," she replies with a daring grin.

I've grown accustomed to that rebellious little daredevil girl in our years of friendship. Story isn't like most girls around here. She's smart as a whip and tough as one too. Sure, there are a lot of farm girls who can hold their own, but none of them are as bold or fearless as Story.

She's the first to leap from the bridge into the lake. The first to jump her bike off of my homemade ramp. And the first to choose dare when everyone else chooses truth. I like that most about her, though I'll never tell her that. She'd slug me on the arm if I ever got sentimental with her. For now, I am content to be the boy she saves her fire for.

I squint into the darkness, and sure enough, a mama opossum and her seven babies stare back at us. I smile. "That's cool, Stor. How'd you stumble across this?"

"I was taking the long way home from school today and saw her running through the brush with her babies hanging all over her back. I picked up my pace and followed them here. Aren't they cute?" she squeals quietly. "Did you know that opossums don't choose to play dead; it's an automatic thing that happens when they feel threatened?" She pushes her glasses up her nose, framing her twinkling eyes.

Her fun facts make me happy inside. "That's awesome," I reply. My eyes track from the nest to the horizon and up to the stars. "We got a nice clear night," I whisper, sitting on a log.

"Yeah, we do," she says, clicking off her flashlight as she joins me.

The nearby creek babbles as it flows away from us into the dark, and for the longest time we just sit with our eyes up and our jaws slacked open. The nights out here in the country are black as coal and the Milky Way shows like glitter in a dustpan. It's the most beautiful thing I've ever seen. Well, besides her.

"Do you think that other places in the world have stars this good?" I ask quietly.

"I'm not sure. But I'd love to find out."

That's my Story. Always wanting adventure. She has a gypsy soul that's born to wander, and as soon as she found out what a bucket list was, she filled a piece of notebook paper front and back. That's the only thing different about us two. I've seen a lot of the world already because my dad is in the Navy. We move every year or two and I get sick of it real fast.

The world is beautiful, no doubt. But the cities are crowded and too bright at night. And about the time I'd make a friend, we'd pick up and move again. So, when the opportunity arose to move in with my grandparents, I jumped at the chance.

I crave deep, long-lasting roots somewhere like Ma and Pa Dixon. They bought their little farm after they got married and have stayed put for forty-five years and counting. That's what I want too.

When Story made me write my own bucket list along with her, it only had six items on it:

1. Be a farmer like Pa Dixon.

2. Work hard with the sun every day.

3. Be smart like my mama.

4. Get respect from my daddy.

5. Marry my best friend.

6. Have a bunch of kids and dogs.

I know that seems silly, but to a kid who never stayed anywhere long enough to make a best friend, it's a big deal. Story laughed when she saw how simple mine was, but she loved me for it anyhow. She knows me deep inside and how much I hate saying goodbye to people I meet along the way. So, my short list makes sense.

After that day, though, I wonder if I'll ever be the kind of man

Story would want. She craves the adventure we only read about in books, and I'm content to stay in Nebraska forever.

That doesn't matter as kids, though. We find excitement every day on the farm and in the creek running through town. But deep down, what I fear more than anything else, is the day that wouldn't be enough for her anymore. She'll leave me behind to go cross off her list.

I sigh into the warm night air. "I think you found the perfect spot to sit and think."

She smiles at me.

I'm not sure what love is, but I imagine it feels something like what I feel inside my chest at this moment. She's the only girl I'll ever be seen with around town; the only person on the planet who knows everything about me. I can trust her with any secret. I'm the luckiest kid in the world.

"You're right, Lukie."

No one else gets to call me 'Lukie' but her, and she loves it.

"This should be our thinking spot," she whispers. "What do you think?"

"That's perfect."

SEVEN

Story

The heat enveloped us as we walked out of the airport into paradise. After a whole day's worth of airplanes and layovers, we finally made it to Nassau with just enough time to settle in and watch the sun take a dip into the ocean.

Luke took a deep breath in and squinted his eyes. "Well, the first thing I want to do is get rid of these boots and jeans." He laughed. "It's hotter than the hinges on the gates of Hell here, and it's evenin' time."

I burst out laughing. "Well, let's at least get to our hotel first, or you're bound to cause a stir with that tour group over there," I said, grabbing his arm and leading him to our taxi.

Checking into the honeymoon suite with Luke was weird, to say the least. The front desk lady kept calling us Mr. and Mrs. Michaels, and I wasn't sure whether to play along or correct her. I chose to smile awkwardly because that was what I did in uncomfortable situations. Luckily, Luke took the reins and was the adult in the situation while I stood there like a rubber ducky. The whole thing made me want to run and hide.

The walk to our room wasn't much better.

The wheels of the bellman's cart clicking on the terra-cotta tile floors was the only thing that broke the silence. When the bellman opened the door for us, I robotically tipped him, and we shuffled inside with our bags. I held my breath as I surveyed the room. Everything about it set the mood for romance. Yet here I was, a non-newlywed, but pretending to be one, and I felt like a complete phony.

I wouldn't want to go through this with anyone but Luke, but this room was meant for me and Dane, and I was having a hard time compartmentalizing that.

A bucket of expensive champagne sat on ice next to a platter of chocolate-covered strawberries, and rose petals covered the floor and bed. The gauzy drapes filtered warm orange and yellow sunset lighting, filling the room with golden light. Perfectly plumped pillows screamed romance in our faces.

Luke and I hadn't talked about our feelings for each other at all before my wedding day, so this was like trying to drink from a firehose without getting wet.

He whistled through his teeth. "Man, this is the ritziest hotel room I've ever seen," he said, rubbing his neck.

He looked as uncomfortable as I felt.

"Leave it to Dane—only wanting the best," I said sarcastically. "This may not be our speed exactly, but we can still enjoy it, right?"

"Damn straight we can. Startin' with these fancy strawberries," he said and took a bite of one. He handed another to me. "They don't taste quite like Ma Dixon's from her garden, but they're pretty good." He glanced at the large French doors that sat slightly ajar. "And look at that. We can walk right down to the beach from our patio. Can't get much better than that, right?"

My throat tightened around a sadness for what I thought my life was going to be. I'd never cared about fancy stuff, but standing in the hotel room I was supposed to be sharing with the husband-who-didn't-happen, hurt. I blinked furiously. The last thing I wanted was for Luke to see my disappointment.

When his arm wrapped around my shoulder, I realized there was no use pretending to be okay. He always knew.

"I get that me bein' here isn't what you were expectin', Stor. If you need me to just buzz off so you can wallow, I completely understand. I'll pick up the pieces if you want, or I can help you save face in front of the people who keep congratulatin' us on our weddin'. The choice is yours. I have no expectations of anything. Even now that you know I have feelin's for you, we don't need to address it now, or ever if you don't want to. I'm just a shoulder you can cry on, someone to rub aloe on you when you've spent too much time in the sun, and a drinkin' buddy. You let me know what you need from me, and I'll be it, okay?"

His soft hazel eyes read me like an open book. I felt like a complete mess while he was so stalwart and strong. "I'm glad you came with me. How would I have done this alone?"

"Ah, you don't give yourself enough credit, Stor." He waved a hand in dismissal. "You're tougher than half the guys in Little Creek, and they all know it too. You can do hard things. And you can lean on me if you want. Just like when we were kids. I had your back then, and I have it now too."

The floodgates I'd been holding back burst, and I crumpled to the floor. He grabbed a blanket from the sofa and placed it over my shoulders before he sat alongside me.

"Most of the time, I've handled this better than I thought I would. But there's so much uncertainty ahead of me now. And that feels so overwhelming," I sobbed.

"Well, then, meet 'em as they come and before you know it, you'll be through 'em."

I took a deep breath and wiped my eyes. "I'm so embarrassed."

"I know."

"Everyone in town'll be talking about this forever. This is one more thing for them to use in their arsenal of gossip. I can already see their expressions and hear hushed voices as I wander into places now. I will never live this down … And what about my job? How am I supposed to go back to work to prying eyes, and see Dane every day and not let it bother me?"

"Take 'em one at a time, Stor. You're not in Little Creek, and you're not in Chicago. You're here in Nassau, and no one knows us from Adam. They aren't whisperin', and if they are, it's 'cause you're so beautiful."

The way he mispronounced Nassau, like 'lasso' in that country-boy drawl, shined a tiny ray of sunshine through my cloudy mood.

He adjusted to a cross-legged position and grinned. "Interrogation or humiliation?" he asked with mischief in his eyes.

I surrendered with a sigh. The last thing I needed to admit was the difficult truth I was already grappling with. "Humiliation," I replied.

And before I knew it, Luke Dixon had me jumping on that fancy bed. Its fluffy pillows and flower petals flew everywhere, and the beautiful silk sheets wrinkled under our feet as we giggled and screamed like kids. It felt so good to ruin the perfection of it all.

I picked up a pillow and whacked him with it. He lost his balance and fell backward against the headboard. I threw myself down next to him and laughed until my sides hurt as he said "Nassau" over and over again without getting it right. It was the kind of laugh you need after a long bout of sorrow. The kind that lifts your spirits and makes your face hurt. The kind I needed in that moment. And it filled the cracks of my broken heart with golden flecks of gratitude.

"I'm so lucky to have you," I said as I wrapped my arms tightly around his strong body. And I meant it.

EIGHT

Story

Junior Year of High School

I look around the circle of teenagers sitting in Liz's dimly-lit family room. We outgrew immature birthday party games, yet here we are. Although now, we moved on from Red Rover and Red Light, Green Light, and replaced them with Spin the Bottle and Truth or Dare. So at least Liz's parties have grown up along with us.

Liz grins in the candlelight. "Are we ready?"

A bunch of us nod our heads, so Liz pulls a name from the jar in the center.

"Ben, truth or dare?"

"Always choose dare," he replies. "That's my mantra."

"Okay," Liz says thoughtfully. "Run shirtless to the neighbor's house down the road—wearing my mom's apron—and ask for a cup of sugar."

"That's easy," Ben says, peeling off his shirt. He throws a flowery apron around his waist and ties it in the back.

As Ben takes off out the door, I see Luke shake his head out of the corner of my eye, and I know exactly what he's thinking. We talked before about how Ben finds any excuse to take his shirt off in front of girls. Luke meets my gaze and a knowing smile tugs at one corner of his mouth. I love how he doesn't need to say a word for me to hear his voice in my head.

"Ben's muscles are a crutch for his bad personality," Luke said to me once. I laughed out loud then, and I stifle a laugh now. Luke knows it and milks my misery by letting a grin completely take over his face, raising his eyebrows. I snort a giggle out of my nose and look away.

Liz turns to me and pulls the jar into her lap. "Story, you're next. Truth or dare?"

"Wait a second, you didn't draw my name. You can't do that, it's cheating."

"Nope. It's my game, I get to change the rules anytime I want to," Liz insists.

Everyone's eyes fall on me. "Fine," I say. I go against my normal choice. "Truth, I guess."

"I want to ask this question, Liz." Jenna Manning interrupts. "Story, how do you really feel about Luke?" A huge grin crosses her face.

I know exactly what she's doing, because she's been trying to tear me and Luke apart for a while now. Jenna started liking Luke in the seventh grade, and soon after, her bullying of me began. This is just another one of her mean little jabs, I'm sure of it. But forcing me to admit to everyone that I have a crush on my childhood best friend by painting me into a corner is a new low, even for her.

My palms begin to sweat and my heart pounds in my ears. I push my glasses up the bridge of my nose, sigh, and look at Luke. He pops his knuckles, avoiding my gaze. I'm pretty sure he's as uncomfortable as I am, because Mama and Ma are always insisting we date each other. It's exhausting. I want that more than anything, but aside from the things Liz and Luke include me in, I don't generally get to sit with the 'cool kids' at school. And although I know he isn't ashamed of me, I'm not sure he'd rebel enough against societal norms to be outwardly interested in a girl like me. He never seems to care about that stuff but has a lot of pressure from those who do.

Jenna, the captain of the cheer squad, has been trying for years to win his heart, and I wonder how long it'll be before she gets what she wants.

Luke and I don't discuss our love lives all that much. It's a topic of conversation I want to bring up, but never have the courage to do so.

The truth is, I love Luke with my whole heart, but I can't risk losing what we have. What if I tell him how I feel and things go south? That's enough motivation to keep quiet. I'm fully prepared to go to my grave carrying the torch I have for him, and that isn't about to change now. So, I press my lips together and take a deep breath with every intention of lying through my teeth.

As I open my mouth, Ben bursts through the door, completely out of breath, with a whole plate of cookies in his hand.

"Mrs. Poulsen did me one better than a cup of sugar! These bad boys are hot out of the oven, and she sent one for each of us!"

Everyone clambers to their feet and rushes toward the warm cookies. Mrs. Poulsen has a reputation of being the best baker in town, and she loves living up to it. Every time we visit, she has something yummy to feed us.

I say a silent thank you to Mrs. Poulsen for bailing me out of this pickle and grab a warm snickerdoodle.

Luke walks up behind me and leans over my shoulder to grab one too. His strong, farmer-boy chest grazes my back, sending a flash of adrenaline through me. I want to crawl out of my skin and hide from Liz and her dumb game, from Jenna and her nosy questions, and from Ben and his shirtless cookie offering. But most of all, I want to hide from Luke. I shouldn't want the one person I can never have. But I do. Badly. And I know one day the secret I carry will eat me alive.

"You seem a bit nervous there, Stor," he teases, jabbing my ribs.

"They might as well call this game Interrogation or Humiliation 'cause that's exactly what it feels like," I mumble under my breath.

Luke laughs out loud and puts his arm around me. "I think

that's a way better name for it." He pulls me aside and leans in close to whisper in my ear. *"I've always hated these stupid games at parties."*

My heart kicks up a notch from trot to full-on gallop.

"Let's ditch out and go home. We can pop some popcorn, watch a movie—your choice—and forget this whole night ever happened. How does that sound?"

Now he's speaking my language. A night in, just the two of us? Yes, please! *"Okay, but how do we get out of here without anyone noticing?"*

"Leave that to me," he whispers and winks at me. *"I'll meet you out front in three minutes. Hustle now, or Liz will insist you make good on your interrogation."*

I slip out the back door just as I hear Luke say loudly, "Hey, Ben, how many pushups can you do again?"

I giggle to myself as I bolt through the darkness.

Three minutes of waiting in the shadow of the garage feels like an eternity as the warm Nebraska night embraces me. The cicadas and frogs harmonize in full force at an almost deafening volume.

Luke sneaks up behind me and makes me squeal. Luckily, that symphony of nature drowns out most of it.

We run full-bore down the street to his truck, laughing like kids the entire way. I've never been so grateful to have been late to a party, having had to park way down the street, than I am right now. We reach the truck, out of breath, hearts on fire, with smiles that cover our whole faces. We did it. We broke out of Alcatraz, and no one even noticed.

We jump in the truck, fling the doors shut, and before I even buckle my seat belt, we're off in a cloud of dust on the way to Ma and Pa Dixon's.

Luke looks over at me and smiles, his eyes twinkling with mischief in the dim radio glow. "Now that was fun!" he says, laughing.

"Liz will never forgive me," I say, still trying to catch my

breath. "But thank you. I needed a distraction to wriggle out of that one."

"That's what friends are for, right?"

Friends. *That awful, yet wonderful word has become loaded with meaning as Luke and I grow up.*

"Yeah. That's what friends are for. And I guess I owe ya one, Luke Dixon. 'Cause you saved my bacon tonight."

NINE

Story

The light crept in through the curtains the next morning, and I rolled over to find Luke asleep on the sofa across the room.

"Always a gentleman," I whispered as I climbed out of bed and smoothed the covers back into place.

I put my favorite country playlist on just loud enough that I could hear it over the shower as it poured over me, but quiet enough not to disturb Luke. I swear, he hasn't slept past the sunrise since he was eight years old, and if anyone deserved the rest, it was him.

Halfway through washing my hair, I paused as my voice echoed around me. For the first time since my wedding, I was singing in the shower instead of crying. A thread of hope sewed together a tiny crack in my heart, and I began to breathe a little easier. I toweled off, dressed, and grabbed my makeup bag to take out onto the patio. There was no way I could resist that cute cafe table calling my name. As I rounded the corner, I found Luke sitting on the bed grinning.

"What?" I asked with suspicion in my voice.

"You make your bed in hotel rooms?" he asked, chuckling.

"What's wrong with that? I don't like making the housekeepers do it every day. They have enough on their plates than to have to come in and make my bed when I can easily do it myself."

Luke smiled. "Yeah, but then you don't get those fun towel animals they make or the fancy mints on the pillows."

"I didn't realize you were a fan of towel animals and fancy mints."

"Me either. 'Til I saw that monkey they made and hung from the towel rack. Now I'm hooked. I gotta see what else they can do. Also, I ate both of our mints from last night's pillow fight. I found them on the floor this mornin' and decided finder's keepers."

I laughed and messed up the bed. "Fine, you win. I'll take the Do Not Disturb sign from the door so they'll come gussy up the room."

"Thank you. I appreciate the gesture." He smiled.

The timing was all wrong to be in paradise with Luke, that was for sure, and I needed lots of time to recover from what happened with Dane. But I also couldn't ignore that my heart sped up a bit as I looked at his fresh morning face. The old feelings I had for him found sunlight and sprouted up through the hole I buried them in.

"I guess we ought to clear the evidence that you slept on the couch, then," I said, grabbing the pillow and blanket he used and tossing them onto the bed. "Otherwise, the maids may think there's trouble in paradise. I'm not sure if there's any punishment for people faking to be newlyweds and staying in the honeymoon suite. What if they kick us out?" I teased.

"Uh-oh. Then we'll have to sleep on the beach under the stars."

"Actually, that doesn't sound half bad. But how could I be sure no critters will get me while I sleep?"

Luke laughed. "You are the toughest woman I know, yet you're still afraid of critters. I guess you gotta have a flaw somewhere."

My heart warmed my entire chest. It was nice to see that

someone I thought so highly of reflected that same admiration back at me—though I felt completely undeserving of it.

"Oh, now." I waved a hand in dismissal. "You're one of the only people in the world who knows all my ugly parts. And it's far worse than being afraid of bugs and spiders."

"And yet, I can't recall a single one of 'em. Except now I gotta add that you make your bed in a hotel room to the list. That's just weird."

I smacked his arm playfully. "You're weird, towel animal lover! Now go get in the shower while I put my makeup on outside and we'll get breakfast at the restaurant."

"Yes, ma'am," he said, rubbing his arm. "I wouldn't want to get on your bad side today. Oh, and hey, Stor? Will you send me that playlist you sang along to at the top of your lungs while you were in here? I kinda liked it, even if it was out of tune," he teased as he stepped through the bathroom doorway.

I tossed the towel from my wet hair at him and it hit him in the face.

His muffled laugh came from underneath. "Mmmm. This smells nice. I just might sneak your shampoo so I can smell like a tropical rainforest too."

"Just stay away from my razor! That cowboy stubble of yours will dull it in two seconds!" I shouted as the door latched closed.

"I make no promises!" he shouted back and started the shower.

The morning sun warmed my shoulders and felt good on my face as I applied my makeup. Tropical flowers and ferns hung all around the patio, and the hum of nature busying around me stilled my soul. I took in a deep, fragrant breath and sighed. The salty ocean air filtered through my nose and into my lungs, and the way it clung to my senses made me feel more alive than I had in years.

"If I'm going to be at rock bottom, it might as well be in a place like this," I whispered to the double hammock that hung between two palm trees.

I finished my mascara, ran a brush through my partially dried hair, and headed toward the water. The serenade of the waves called to me, so, as if in a trance, I followed its song down the little path through the trees until I found the beach.

As I came to the clearing where the foliage ended and the beach began, my mouth dropped open. I'd seen the ocean before, but not one this turquoise blue yet transparent all at the same time. If my soul were a color, I imagined it would look just like that: a reflection of God's eyes.

The tide had already gone out and left behind tiny little sea treasures and shells on the sand. I picked up a few, rinsed them in the surf, and put them into my pocket to save.

I heard a voice behind me. "Wow. Have you ever in your life seen water like this before?" Luke marveled.

His dark hair was wet and combed and he smelled like toothpaste and aftershave. And possibly a hint of my shampoo, too.

"I haven't seen the ocean since I was a boy. But I sure don't remember it bein' this pretty."

"I know, right? I've never seen anything like it. You can see way down to the bottom. Look. Over there is a whole school of fish hanging out." I pointed a few yards out and stared in awe.

"We should get some snorkelin' gear and explore it today," Luke said as he kicked off his flip-flops and pulled me down with him to sit in the sand.

"I'd like that," I said, scooting close to him so our shoulders touched.

After a few minutes of silence, I spoke up again, "That big fancy wedding I almost had was a bit much for my taste. I felt so much pressure from Dane to spend a ton of money and have the whole shebang. Guess what I *really* wanted."

"What?"

"A small wedding in the big red barn on Fourth Street with a few close family and friends. I always pictured a sunset ceremony with the barn doors flung open and a thousand twinkling lights hung everywhere. I wanted to wear my cowgirl boots under my dress while holding a wildflower bouquet."

"Your weddin' was none of that," Luke replied.

"Right? That should've been a huge clue that I wasn't good enough for Dane when the wedding of my dreams was ridiculous to him." I scooped up a handful of sand and watched it sift through my fingers. "Next time around, I don't want anything extravagant. I want the complete opposite."

"Like a drunken weddin' at a drive-through in Vegas?" Luke asked with a laugh.

"Well, maybe not *that* far on the opposite end of the spectrum. More like..." I paused to think. "Bare feet in the sand. Sunset on the beach. Just me and him. On my way down to our spot I'd pick a tropical flower to hold or put it behind my ear. We'd grab some random strangers off the street to be our witnesses, and the ceremony would be quick and simple. The sound of the ocean would be the only music playing. That's what I would choose to do."

"Why the change of heart? It's not too late to have your dream country weddin'," Luke said softly.

"I know. But it was so much planning and stress and money —just so I could get dumped at the altar. The flowers all died, food for three hundred people was expensive, and the wedding cake didn't taste nearly as good as it looked. I want to focus solely on our love next time, and honestly, not even tell anyone we're going to do it. Just fly off on a plane and come back Mr. and Mrs."

Luke smiled and sighed. "I think keepin' it simple is a great idea. Although there would be a lot of angry people when you came back home."

"Eh, they'd get over it," I said, shrugging. "I'm sick of making choices based on how others will feel or what they'll think."

"Atta girl," Luke said and fist-bumped me. "Life is too short to waste on what others think."

Although I agreed, letting go of that people-pleasing habit was going to be hard.

I FOUND myself out in the sand any chance I got, wandering out to the beach like it had some kind of magnetic pull on me. I craved the calm the ocean gave me, and a part of me wanted to stay there forever and never return home—wherever 'home' was.

The prospects of what to do next loomed, leaving me overwhelmed. Luke told me to take it one at a time, like the waves that crashed on the beach. But I still spent way too much energy worrying about the future. And the next thing I knew my shoulders were heavy and my throat was tight. Should I go back to Chicago and continue with the life I'd built for myself, or tuck tail and go back home to Nebraska? There were pros and cons to both. I stood in the middle of a tug o' war between my past and my present, trying to decide what my future should be.

Just as the waves of confusion and despair pulled me under, Luke's voice reached out to me like a life preserver. "Hey. How'd I know I'd find you out here?" He sat down beside me in the sand.

"I guess I'm too predictable," I said, forcing a smile through my tears.

Luke wiped the sand from his hand onto his shorts and caught my tears with his calloused thumb. "What's goin' on in there?" he asked, burrowing deep into my eyes.

"If I said nothing, would you believe me?"

"Not for a second, so you might as well spill the beans."

I sighed heavily and searched for the words. "I don't know where my life is headed. Does Dane leaving me at the altar have to change everything? I'm still a successful accountant—that doesn't change just because he dumped me. But what about the fact that I work with him and will have to see him every day? I'm not looking forward to that. It'll be like pouring salt in a wound all day long.

But I can't avoid him forever; I've got to pick up my things from his apartment at the very least. My lease is up at the end of next month and I've got to decide what I'm going to do next. I'm not sure I want to re-commit to another year in the city."

"Wow. That's a lot to unpack, Stor," Luke said thoughtfully. "If you don't want to re-commit to life in the city, where would you go? Back home to Little Creek?"

"Maybe? But then there's the embarrassment and shame I'd feel because people would think I was a quitter for not sticking it out. Or they'd think I couldn't hack it in the big city."

"Or how 'bout you don't give so much energy to what others will think, and just do what's best for you?"

"That's easier said than done, Luke. Especially coming from the town's golden boy who can do no wrong."

"You don't think I have people in my life who look at me with critical eyes? You must've forgotten about my father. You remember Mr. Navy Man, who would only be proud of me if I followed in his footsteps? And because I'm 'only a farmer' like Pa Dixon, I'm fallin' short of my potential. Remember that guy? And you don't think I hear people whisper around town that I wasted my talent by not playing college ball? You're not the only one they gossip about."

"Oh, Luke. I'm sorry. I didn't mean to insinuate you had it easy. I know you don't. I just feel like the expectations on me are so heavy and I don't know how to hold it all."

"When I struggle on the farm with somethin', Pa shares a story with me that his pa shared with him long ago. He says to me, 'Luke, we aren't meant to go it alone. Like the animals my pa used to work with on his farm, when there's a heavy load to pull, we'd yoke 'em together so they each take some of the burden. That way the job gets easier for everyone involved.'" He rubbed his face and smiled. "We use heavy equipment for most of that nowadays, but the concept still works." He paused and let his words sink in before continuing, "The same's true for people too, Stor. If you yoke up to someone willin' to share your load, the burden gets easier to carry."

I dug my toes into the sand and thought for a bit about his words. Dane would never have been someone I could yoke up to. He told me I was an independent woman who didn't need help, so I always felt guilty and weak when I asked for it. Luke never made me feel bad for needing him. He enjoyed it when I depended on him for things. Even as we sat on the beach, I was a complete mess that'd come apart at the seams, and he just sat there, all even-keeled, listening to me complain. He'd share anything I asked from him willingly. He'd give the shirt off his back to anyone who needed it, and never expect anything in return.

Luke was so much more than his dad gave him credit for. He was the epitome of a good man, and he deserved the utmost respect for that.

"You're right. I honestly don't think Dane would've been the 'yoke up' kind of husband. Maybe I dodged more of a bullet than I realized."

"So, then, let your burdens be shared, Story. You don't have to do all this alone. And for the record, the people of Little Creek aren't nearly as critical of you as *you* are of you. I'm pretty sure you're the only one holdin' yourself to that impossible standard. Most of them love you and want the best for you and would welcome you home with open arms."

"Part of me wants to believe that. The other part of me still feels like I have something to prove to everyone. I spent a lot of my formative years being thrust into a humiliating spotlight and teased. I felt like I had to show everyone I wasn't a joke. Making something of myself was how I did it."

"I mean, I can understand why you'd think that. You did take a lot of slings and arrows growin' up. But the truth is, those you have to prove your worth to, aren't people you want in your cheerin' section anyway. And those who are cheerin' you on from the sidelines already see your worth. So let go of those people who make you feel like you're never good enough—in Little Creek *and* in Chicago. Life is too short to fight for the approval of people who will never give it. Believe me, I know. I've tried my whole life to win the respect of my dad. But deep down, I'll never earn it. And I have to learn how to be okay with that."

"So how do we let go of it, then?"

"That part I'm still workin' on," he said, smiling.

"Maybe we could collaborate and brainstorm a solution. How'd you say it, 'yoke up?'" I nudged his shoulder.

He leaned into me. "I think I'd like that."

"Yeah, me too."

Luke shuffled something sitting in the sand next to him. "Enough of the heavy stuff for a minute, I have a surprise for you," he said, handing me a bag.

"Snorkeling gear!" I squealed as I pulled out my set.

I slipped my goggles on and smiled with squished cheeks.

"Race you to the water!" I said, jumping up and running toward the ocean with the rest of my gear.

Luke fumbled in his flippers behind me, and I laughed as the first wave hit my knees.

Floating above an ocean of creatures that had no care in the world enveloped me with a calmer perspective. Those fish had no idea that life above them was complicated and hard. They just kept swimming. Even when the current tossed them around, they righted themselves without fuss and kept moving. If a fish or a crab could do that, why couldn't I? The riptide that was my life at the moment was tumultuous and chaotic. Yet I could pick myself back up and move forward too. My throat tightened and my chest swelled as tears of gratitude fogged up my goggles and I stood up to clean them off. A wave blasted me from behind, tossing me around. I frantically searched for the surface but couldn't distinguish which way was up. I kicked and fought against it, but the more I did, the harder it became to gain control. My heart raced and just before panic set in, I thought of those fish. I gave into the wave, tumbling until I found the sunlight above. I rolled over to float on my back and gasped at the air when the breeze hit my face. As my pulse returned to normal and my breathing steadied, I focused on the clouds passing lazily overhead. The hot sun warmed my body like a cozy blanket. As the waves clicked and sloshed in my ears, the panic and overthinking that had inundated me before faded away. My shoulders relaxed, my mind slowed, and my lungs expanded, making room for the possibility that after the chaos, everything would be okay.

TEN

Luke

Liz's Birthday Party, Age 13

How I got roped into coming to this party, I'm ashamed to say. There is only one reason I consented to something this silly: Story begged me to come. This is the first co-ed birthday party any of us have ever had, and Story didn't want to come alone. None of us know what to expect, so having each other at least gives some familiarity to the whole thing.

Her emerald-green eyes pulled me under their spell when she asked me to come yesterday on our way home from school. And before I knew it, I heard myself agree. I've gotten into a real bad habit of always saying yes to whatever she asks of me, and it's getting my heart into some trouble, that's for sure.

I'm sitting in the backyard of Story's best friend, Liz's house with a dozen other classmates. Some of them I know, like Jenna Manning, Shane Johnson, and Ben Wilder, and some of them I don't. We stand awkwardly listening to top 40 music—which I hate —on a boombox and sipping Hawaiian Punch. It isn't until Liz's mom feeds us pizza that we all loosen up a bit.

I head inside to use the bathroom and overhear Story, Jenna, *and Liz giggling in the kitchen. Liz's voice accuses Story of liking someone at the party, and I pause in the hallway to eavesdrop like a chump.* There's no way Story likes someone, is there? *She only spends her free time with me and Liz, and I like being the only boy in her life.* Besides, she tells me everything, doesn't she?

"Come on, Story, admit it, you totally like him!"

Jenna's voice joins in. "He is growing up nicely."

"Well," Story *replies in a girly tone I never heard before, "It's not that I like* like *him, but lately he's kinda caught my eye a little more."*

"I knew it!" Liz shouted. "We've gotta get you two to kiss!"

"No way!" Story protests. "He doesn't think of me like that, because if he did, he would've 'fessed up by now, don't you think?"

"Of course he doesn't think of you like that," Jenna says, laughing.

"What's that supposed to mean?" Story asks, sounding hurt.

Yeah, Jenna, what's that supposed to mean? *I think.*

"He's one of the hottest guys at school," Jenna defends. "And you're ..." she trails off. "You just don't fit."

Liz dismisses Jenna's comment and tries to smooth things over.

"It could be that he's just scared. Come on, Stor. I'll start a game of Spin the Bottle and if the stars align, you'll get your chance."

"And what if I don't?"

"Eh." Liz shrugged. "You'll get some kissing practice in, at least. So, when you do finally get the nerve, you'll know how." Liz giggled.

"If you don't want the chance to kiss him, I'll take it," Jenna prods.

"Fine, I'll do it," I hear Story say.

I rush outside before they see me hiding in the hallway.

I stand on the patio and look around the yard. My goal is to size up which lucky jerk she was talking about and plot how I can punch his nose and make it look like an accident. Or maybe a game of Red Rover will do the trick, then I can 'innocently' clothesline him and knock him flat on his back.

Liz squeezes through the doorway with an empty Coke bottle and corrals everyone toward the patio.

Jenna rubs my arm as she passes me and says low in my ear, "I'll sit next to you, Luke."

But my mind is too preoccupied with what could happen next. What if Story's spin lands on me? Will she be disappointed? Will I be a good kisser? *Story claims all of the girls—especially Jenna—fawn all over me, but I've never shown any interest, much less kissed any of them. She asked me why once, and all I did was shrug and change the subject. I'm not ready to tell her that I want my first kiss to be with her. I'm afraid if we do kiss, it will ruin our friendship, but that doesn't stop me from thinking about it, though. A lot.* It's okay to think about it, right? No harm, no foul.

I'm starting to feel okay about the possibility of getting to kiss Story tonight under the guise of Spin the Bottle, but what if her spin lands on someone else? What if mine does? Could I sit there and watch her kiss another guy and keep a straight face? Definitely not, but I have to try. Faking a stomachache now will make me look like a pansy.

The next thing I know, Story is yanking me backward by the collar into the hallway. She stands crazy close to me, and I struggle to focus on what she's saying because my heart is pounding so loud.

"Liz wants to play Spin the Bottle. I've never kissed anyone before, and I'm afraid I'll mess up. What if I flop and everyone laughs at me?"

My throat tightens and I clear it to get rid of the nerves piling up. "So, what do you want me to do? Suggest a different game? You want to sneak out and leave?"

That's exactly what I want to do. I don't want to watch Story kiss someone else, and I don't want to be kissing another girl either. We can run off right now and keep everything perfect between us forever.

"No, silly! I want you to practice with me real quick," she whispers.

"You want me to do what?" *I ask a little too loudly. My wild heart bucks me off and leaves me behind, bruised and sitting in the dirt.*

"Ssshhh! They'll hear us," she says, looking over her shoulder. "Hurry and kiss me! Neither of us have ever done it before, and we're best friends, so we'll probably be each other's first kiss eventually."

Ho-ly Toledo. Are my ears hearing her right? *My insides burst out the gate like an angry bull in a rodeo, and immediately my hands start sweating. I think my hesitation makes her nervous, because she turns on the charm I can't resist.*

"Please? I don't want to look stupid," she pleads with puppy-dog eyes and a flirty smile.

And really, how can I even think about saying no? It's like she's giving me everything I've ever wanted.

"I mean, are you sure? How can we be sure either of us are any good at it?"

"I don't know. But you're my best friend, and I'm yours, and that'll never change. There's no safer way to do it."

I fight to hold my grin from running off the sides of my face at the prospect of finally kissing Story. All I can come up with in reply that doesn't give away my excitement is, "Yeah, sure. Okay."

Then she kisses me. Right here in the darkened hallway at Liz's house. Right next to their dusty family photos on the wall, with Liz's parents watching TV two doors down. It all happens so fast; I barely know what's going on.

Our mouths don't line up right, she hits more of my chin than my lips. I'm caught completely off-guard, so I know I'm bad at it. I want a redo, but stupid Liz hollers from the back door for us to hurry up, and that's it. Story runs off without even looking back.

I have no idea what she's even thinking, and that's never happened between us. She disappears and leaves me discombobulated with my pulse racing and heart in my throat. I hate that the whole thing is over before it even began.

I resolve right then and there, if I ever get the chance to kiss her again, it'll be the best kiss of her life.

ELEVEN

Story

"Luke!" I whispered as I shook him from his slumber. "Wake up, I've got to tell you something."

"Huh? What?" He stirred, trying to make sense of his confusion.

"I have a confession," I said as sweetly as I could, knowing I'd be in trouble for what I'd done.

"What'd you do now, Stor?" he asked, tipping his cowboy hat back down over his eyes and settling in.

"So, after my run this morning, I may have signed us up for The Newlywed Game today," I said with a grimace.

"Now why would you go and do that?"

"'Cause the winners get a free day trip to Big Major Cay to swim with the pigs and I *really* want to go."

"Stor, why would we come all the way to Nassau to swim with pigs, when we can do it on the farm for free? I could turn a sprinkler on ... The pigs would love it."

I grinned. I'd never get sick of the way he mispronounced Nassau. *Oh. My. Heart.* I pulled his hat from his face and leaned in close. "'Cause here we get to do it in gorgeous aqua water and not in the smelly mud like back home. Plus, it's been on my bucket list since I was in high school ..." I trailed off.

Luke cracked one eye open and looked at me. His sigh said it all: he'd do it for me, but he wouldn't necessarily like it.

I squealed with excitement and kissed his forehead before putting his hat back over his eyes. "Thanks, Lukie! We're bound to win. There's no way the other couples know each other as well as we do. Lifelong best friends for the win," I said over my shoulder as I ran off to shower.

THAT EVENING we wandered down to the amphitheater for the competition. The crowds were starting to file in and find their seats, so just before we walked through the archway into the tropical oasis that surrounded the stage, I stopped Luke.

"Now, remember. We are a regular newlywed couple. Don't hesitate to act like it, okay?"

A smile tugged at the corners of his mouth before he spoke, "What did you have in mind, Stor?"

"Well, we need to *look* like newlyweds."

"And how exactly do you plan to do that?"

"For starters, we should walk in holding hands. And when we sit down, you should put your arm around me," I said in a hushed voice so our plan wouldn't be overheard.

"Anything else?"

"Just act like I'm your wife, silly." I laughed and smacked his arm playfully.

"I can manage that," he said as he laced his fingers through mine and led me through the crowd toward the check-in table.

But the feelings that came along with that simple gesture hit me like a freight train. I was a newly-dumped, not a newlywed, yet my heart didn't feel broken at all. His calloused hands fit perfectly around mine, and I found myself appreciating the way they defined his work ethic without him having to say a word. He instinctively caressed my knuckle with his thumb. I felt more at home in that small gesture than I did in Dane's rose-filled rooftop proposal in the city.

A kaleidoscope of butterflies erupted inside, and all I could focus on was how good it felt to hold Luke's hand. Then, my train of thought ran off the rails, caught fire, and plummeted into a ravine as I wondered how it would feel to kiss his lips after all these years, since holding his hand was this amazing. And I'm not talking about the quick, barely-there kiss I planted on him in Liz's hallway when we were thirteen. Like a *real* kiss. A kiss with feelings behind it. A we-aren't-just-friends-anymore kiss.

When the woman at the check-in table asked our names, I internally thanked Luke for being able to come up with a straight answer. After losing myself in that lovely little daydream, I sure couldn't.

He led me to a small loveseat on the stage situated between four others and we sat down. Close. Like, *thisclose.* His arm stretched behind me and rested on my shoulders, and not only did I feel at home with his affection, but I felt safe too. He was like a warm, hard-bodied, safe haven from a storm of emotions—something else I never experienced with Dane. I closed my eyes to take in everything swirling around inside and took a deep, steadying breath.

Luke's lips brushed against my ear and set my whole left side ablaze as he whispered, "You okay?"

My goosebumps had goosebumps at this point, and my reply was strangled in my throat. I managed a feeble nod and, "Mmmhmm," escaped unscathed, but nothing else sensible would present itself. Then I made the huge mistake of actually making eye contact with him.

His sincere hazel eyes searched mine for answers to questions he hadn't even asked, and I was instantly exposed and out in the open. A deer caught in the crosshairs, with nowhere to escape to. But the craziest thing happened: I didn't want to run and hide like I did when I'd see my bully coming down the hallway through a sea of students.

Or when I ran into Jenna Manning and her mom at the department store and my mom *insisted* on talking to "my friend from school." No. This time I knew I was safe. Luke's arm around me and his familiar gaze took me home to a porch swing at sunset. I wanted to be defenseless, which was weird and new for me. *How had I been best friends with this man for twenty years and never knew he could disarm me like that?*

"You've got a whole lot goin' on in there," he whispered, sending more chills down my arms. "It's not a great time to talk about it right now, but can we later?"

I nodded dumbly again and forced a smile as the rest of the couples filed in and sat down.

"Okay, good. But for now, Stor, we gotta up our game. You can't just sit there and nod. You gotta answer questions in order to win the pig swimmin' thing. You with me?" He cracked a huge smile and stroked my knuckle.

How was he so cool and calm? I was basically on fire, and he was easy like Sunday morning.

"Yes. I'm with you," I said with itty bitty baby confidence. *But, hey, words finally came out, so that was a small win!* I cleared my throat and settled into his side.

"Atta girl. Now let's win this thing," he said into my hair, punctuating it with a small kiss.

Man, he wasn't pulling any punches. Once he got the green light to act like a couple, he grabbed my hand and ran me straight into Luke Land. I never wanted to leave.

"Welcome to The Newlywed Game!" the host said enthusiastically into a microphone.

The applause of the crowd cleared the fog around me, and I snapped into competition mode.

"I will ask a series of questions and the couple with the highest points wins an excursion to Pig Beach. Each of you has a dry-erase board and a marker to write down your answers. If your answers match up, you get five points. After five rounds, we will add up the points and announce the winner," the host said, waving for the crowd to applause again.

After introducing each of the couples, and making us turn in our seats to face each other, he began with an easy question, "Question number one: Who said I love you first?"

My mind flashed back to my wedding day and finding Luke's letter, then the conversation in the courtyard that followed. I furiously wrote *Luke* on my board and held it tightly against my chest.

Luke wrote his answer just as quickly. His eyes sparkled with excitement as we waited.

When it was time to flip our boards over, every couple racked up five points.

"Question number two is for the guys: What is your wife's favorite movie?"

This was a no-brainer. I had made him watch *Princess Bride* with me a million times since we were kids.

Luke snickered and bit the cap from his marker with his teeth and wrote his answer down.

Another five points ticked onto the board, but only for three of us. A bubble of excitement welled up inside me.

The host asked the next question, "Question number three is for the ladies: What was your husband's first car?"

And suddenly, I was riding shotgun in Luke's old F-150. It was an unspoken rule that we sang at the top of our lungs to the silly mixed CDs I made. Laying in the bed of that truck, we talked about our deepest dreams while looking at the stars—just the two of us. Always. It was from that spot in the passenger seat that I first started to love Luke. I could still see the glow of the radio highlighting his strong jaw and perfectly imperfect smile. It was in that spot that I tucked him into a tiny pocket of my heart where heartbreak and complication couldn't touch us. Because I was convinced my love for him would always go unrequited, and I would've rather loved him quietly inside than lose him altogether.

"Three more seconds to answer," the host said into the microphone, snapping me back to the present.

I scribbled *F-150* on my board right before the timer buzzed and earned us another five points.

Luke's eyes sparkled as he smiled at me from across the couch. He remembered like I did how valuable that beat-up old truck was to us both. It was like the inside joke that only we understood, and we connected to it at a depth no one else could.

"Question number four: Who is the better driver?"

We both scrawled out Luke's name on our boards and I shook my head and laughed. There was a reason he called me Granny when I drove. We both knew, hands-down, he was more skilled behind the wheel.

Five more points for team Dixon.

"The final question, folks," the host announced with tension in his voice. "We have two couples here that are neck and neck, and this could either tie it up or win it."

I took a deep breath and smiled at Luke. His face brimmed with confidence, and it made me feel proud to be his ... whatever we were now.

"Question number five: Which of you is more successful?"

I thought for a moment. Should I have written what *I* thought or what I thought Luke would write? I sat across from him, thinking about how hard he worked, and how he was such a pillar of kindness in the community back home. There was no contest in who was more successful. Sure, I made more money, but Luke Dixon was goodness in a mason jar. With only a few seconds to spare, I wrote Luke's name down and hugged my board.

The look on his face when we flipped our answers around was one of confusion and amusement. His board said my name. My board said his.

The couple we were neck and neck with had now tied with us.

"Ladies and gentlemen, we have a tie," the host announced. "There is only one way we do tiebreakers around here, and that's with a kiss-off."

The crowd erupted.

Or was that my nerves? Holy cow. I hadn't kissed Luke in over a decade, and that wasn't my finest work. *By far.* What if I still sucked at kissing Luke? And this time it'd be in front of a big crowd, instead of in a dark hallway. My mind reeled, my heart pounded in my chest and my palms began to sweat. I could feel the panic settling in, until I looked at Luke.

His calm smile set me at ease, but the inferno that blazed in his eyes piqued my curiosity. Suddenly, this was no longer about winning first prize, but about figuring out what was going on inside Luke Dixon's head.

My eyes questioned his as he led me to the front of the stage along with the host and the other couple. His poker face was solid, and he held his cards close to his vest.

"Now, a kiss-off is determined by the amount of applause the crowd gives each couple. The louder the audience's reaction to each kiss determines who wins. Understood?" The host turned to us.

We nodded.

"So, vote with your applause, audience. This one's for you."

The rival couple was up first. I had to admit, they had great chemistry, and the audience responded accordingly.

Luke and I knew everything about each other, we had that part in the bag. But did we have what it took to make a crowd go wild? Based on our thirteen-year-old first kiss, I seriously doubted it. I didn't even hit his lips properly at Liz's house that night, then I ran off like a coward.

I had about given up hope that we could win when Luke's fingertips brushed mine. I grabbed onto him like a lifeline and waited for the wave of panic to pass.

Luke leaned in close to my ear and whispered, "Remember the last time we kissed?"

I nodded numbly, staring into the crowd.

"Well, this one will be nothing like that."

The host announced our turn.

Luke wrapped his farm arms around me, tipped me backward, and kissed me. Not like a sweet, tender, church kiss, but a passionate kiss that had been simmering beneath the surface for years. The kind that would've made my grandma clutch her pearls. The kind that the ladies at the beauty salon would've called, 'indecent.' The exact kind of kiss that had all the chemistry I had always hoped for but never experienced.

As his hungry lips explored mine, I understood why cartoons saw fireworks and had hearts shooting out of their eyes afterward. *Wowza*. He started me on fire and stood back to watch me burn. I was ash in his hands, and that was all I could ever hope to be again. But I had a choice to make: melt in his arms or give it to him right back.

I ran my fingers up his shoulders and into his dark hair and returned the fervor. The sound of satisfaction that came from him told me I was on the right track, so I pressed onward. I barely heard the whistling and applause from the crowd. The only thing that brought me back to Earth was the tap on my shoulder. The host announced that we had clearly won. But suddenly, winning the grand prize excursion played second fiddle to what had happened between Luke and me. That kiss was etched into my mind like the initials we carved into a tree when we were ten.

After the game, we collected our excursion vouchers and headed back to our suite. A loaded silence hung between us, and I wasn't sure how to address it. Luckily for me, Luke broke the ice first.

"So, what now?" he asked with an uncomfortable chuckle as we reached our stop.

I unlocked the door, swung it wide open, and shoved him inside.

TWELVE

Luke

The minute the door clicked shut, Story's emerald eyes ignited, and a sexy smile swept across her face. She pressed her body against mine, and I stumbled backward against the wall. Our bodies molded together as if they had been created by the same sculptor: two separate creations but made to fit seamlessly. Her heartbeat pounded against my chest, and my own pulse quickened to match it. She messed up my hair while her mouth brushed across mine and down my neck. Her breath left goosebumps in its wake, whispering to my skin words that couldn't be spoken. But Story's lips did more than kiss me. They *exposed* me. I had never in my life been so seen, so known, so *wanted,* as when she poured herself over me. She knew exactly how to unhinge my mind, push me to the brink of undoing, then pull me back from the ledge just before I jumped.

I lost myself in her fire, allowing my fingertips to trace the curve of her hips, the small of her back, her jawline. Her warm, soft skin exploited my need to be close to her. To fulfill the need to make up for lost time. To make sure that this was real. And I pulled her as close as I could to keep my dream alive. I explored her like uncharted territory: cautiously at first, then diving in with reckless abandon. Unleashing the wildfire I dampened for years consumed me so fully I wasn't sure there'd be anything left of me tomorrow. I stood with my toes on the line I had only ever crossed in my head, ready to leap to the other side.

But as her lips became more familiar, something stirred inside me, growing louder the more I ignored it. This was everything I'd ever wanted, and yet deep down I knew it wasn't what we *needed*. Not yet. So, when her hands started pulling at my shirt, I stopped her. How I stopped her was a mystery to me. I deserved saint-hood. Or knighthood. *Or both*. Because somehow, I resisted the irresistible woman.

"Slow down, Stor," my gravelly voice said as I dropped my forehead down and put my shaking hands over hers.

She pulled back slowly. The hurt and confusion in her eyes killed me. I needed to come up with more words to explain, but my heart raced so fast I could barely breathe, much less speak. I led her over to the edge of the bed and sat down.

When she grinned and eagerly joined me, I jumped up like I'd sat on a cactus. *Nope. Not the bed. That makes things worse.*

"Maybe over here," I whispered, taking her hands and pulling her to the couch. *Okay, yes. Nice, neutral ground.* We could sit and face each other with some much-needed space between us.

As she lowered next to me she started to cry.

I was officially the biggest jerk in the whole world. *Words, man! Say something!*

"Luke, I'm so sorry. I misinterpreted what happened at the game and thought you wanted this too." She buried her pretty face in her hands and sobbed. "I feel so stupid!"

I peeled her hands away and tipped her chin up so she would meet my eyes. "Stor, you misinterpreted nothin'. I *do* want this. More than anything else I've ever wanted in my life. More than I want oxygen, for cryin' out loud! *You* are my dream. I've wanted to kiss you and hold you like this for *so* long. But I can't let it happen like this. When you give your body to me, I want to know that your heart and soul are included in the deal. I can't move any further ahead with you without knowin' whether I have the promise that you'll love me forever along with it." My chest heaved and my stomach twisted in knots. *Sainthood, I tell ya.*

"I'm not sure what you mean."

"You're fresh off your engagement bein' broken off, and there's a lot still to sift through with that. I don't want to push you too fast. You need time to heal before you can truly love again. And I need one hundred percent of you, because I've patiently waited for this, and I'll only marry once."

"You ... want to marry me?"

I laughed at the ridiculousness of her question. "Of course I want to marry you. What do you think number five on my bucket list meant?" I pulled out my worn-out list from my wallet.

5. Marry my best friend.

She looked up from my feeble list and her eyes filled with tears again. "I thought that was more of a generalized statement," she said with a weak laugh.

"Nope. It meant you. It has always meant you. And I'll wait as long as I have to make sure I get to cross that one off."

She wiped her eyes and smiled weakly. "I still feel like an idiot for jumping on you like that," she said, looking away.

"Well, don't. This has pretty much been the best day of my whole life, and it's all because I finally got a redo."

"A redo?"

"Yeah. You know, from Liz's party? That has haunted me forever. It was awesome, because you kissed me, but also awful because I wasn't ready and didn't get a chance to join in before it was over. Then you ran off and left me there feelin' like I was draggin' behind a spooked horse."

She laughed—the hearty kind that only I could get out of her, and it was music to my ears. I felt my shoulders relax a bit and I took a big, satisfying breath.

"The truth is, you've always had that effect on me," I said, wiping a stray tear that had run down her cheek. "And I'd go to hell and back if it meant I'd get a chance to love you, for real. But not yet. Not like this, okay?"

"Okay," she agreed with hesitation. "But what about holding hands and kissing? Do we not get to do that anymore?"

The thought of knowing how her lips tasted, and how her hands felt all over me, then retreating into the friend zone sounded impossible. And frankly, I didn't want to do that. *At all.* Not even a little bit. Not after makin' it this far.

"How about, only in public? That way there's no way we'll cross a line we aren't ready for. Deal?"

"Deal," she said, flashing that amazing smile at me.

"Now, if you don't mind, I need to walk this off for a bit. I feel like I've been sucker-punched in a bar fight." I laughed. "Maybe I'll dunk myself in the ocean, too," I said with weak resolve and stood from the couch.

"Sounds good," she said with a laugh. "I think I'll go take a long, hot shower and get ready for bed."

"Not helpin'!" I yelled over my shoulder as I walked out on the patio and disappeared into the darkness.

IT WAS LATE when I returned to our room, but it took quite a while of walking to talk myself into the fact that I'd done the right thing. *Damn, that was rough.* Only one small lamp lit up the room. It highlighted the grumpy scowl she made when she slept, and it made my heart all fuzzy and warm. I wanted more than anything to climb in beside her and wrap her in my arms, because that was where I belonged. But that would be asking the devil for trouble. Instead, I crawled into the hammock on the patio and stared up at the stars for a while. After my heart and mind finally settled down, I tipped my hat down over my eyes and drifted off to sleep.

THIRTEEN

Story

L uke laughed as the pigs swam around him on Pig Beach. They gravitated toward him, which made sense to me; he had a way with every living creature in his life. His gentle strength was magnetizing, and I felt myself drawn closer to it the more time we spent together. He was a rip tide of goodness that I eagerly floated toward.

I watched him as he swirled around and laughed. His farmer's tan had started to even out across his strong chest and arms after days in the sun, but my eyes wouldn't stop staring at his abs. The way they flexed when he laughed turned me inside-out, so I made a fool of myself on purpose to keep it going. Watching Luke Dixon was about as captivating as the scenery in the Bahamas, and just as hot. *No, hotter.*

He scooped up a piglet and held it in his arms, making it squeal and kick like crazy. I couldn't help but smile at the joy on his face. I snapped a photo with my phone and joined him in the water for a few more selfies.

"Well, I'll be damned," he said as I sidled up next to him. "I always knew pigs couldn't fly, but they sure can swim. This is really cool, Stor. Thanks for bringin' this ol' farm boy out to swim with some pigs in the Bahamas." He wrapped his arm around my sun-kissed shoulders, and I leaned into him.

"You'll have to add this to your bucket list just so you can cross it off," I replied, patting a pink nose that swam beside me. "Heaven knows you need more than six things on your list."

Luke kissed the top of my head. "My list is perfect just the way it is. But I'd go on every last adventure with you while you cross off yours." He squinted into the sun and rubbed his pink cheeks. "I don't know about you, but I could use a few minutes in the shade. Let's go lay under the umbrella."

He grabbed my hand, leading me to our spot on the beach. I took off my sunglasses and stretched out on the blanket. After winning a fight with the umbrella, he relaxed on his side next to me.

"Tell me somethin' about you that I don't know," he said softly as his hazel eyes studied my face.

"Hmmm, let me think. Well, I'm the top accountant at my firm because I nailed the Hansen Foods account. Those bonuses alone helped me pay off my car in two years," I said proudly.

"Look at you go!" he said with a grin. "That's really awesome, Stor."

"Well, it helped that I was a farm girl at heart, because the minute I showed up in boots, ready to work, I had Mr. Hansen eating out of the palm of my hand."

"Smart man. But who *wouldn't* love a sweet farm girl like you?" he asked.

My mind wandered back to that business trip and how Dane's words made me feel so small, and I knew exactly who didn't love the farm girl side of me. I forced a smile and sighed.

"Well, you'd be surprised," I said. Before I could sit too long with those memories rushing back to me, I turned the question onto him. "What about you? Tell me something I don't know about you."

He ran a sandy hand through his hair and thought for a

minute. "I turned down three scholarships to play college football after you left."

I raised up on my elbows. "You did *what?* Why?"

"Because playin' football was one of my dad's dreams for me. And when I realized that even *that* wouldn't get me his praise, I walked away from it. All I ever wanted was for him to say he was proud of me, so I subjected my body to torn ligaments, concussions, and broken bones. I learned after high school that it was too high a price."

"Oh, wow. I never knew. Do you ever regret not going to college?"

"Nah." He waved a hand. "I've learned two trades; I can weld *and* fix anything with an engine. And I may not have a master's degree, but I know my way around a farm. I can tell someone exactly what's missin' in the soil by the way their crops look, and I am proud of the work I accomplish in a day. That's gotta count for somethin' right?"

"Absolutely it does. And even without a fancy degree, you're a whole lot smarter than I am," I replied.

He shook his head and smiled. "Now we both know that ain't true."

"Sure, it is. You can feed a nation. I just talk people into giving me their money."

"Imagine what we could accomplish together then," he joked, but his eyes revealed more about that statement than his words ever would.

I raised my chin toward him, and as if on cue he met me halfway. Our lips met with a soft need for acceptance that had always existed between us but went ignored for years. He kissed me with purpose, creating an empire of emotion in one act and searing it into my memory. His fingers traced my jawline, my neck, my skin, leaving me on fire in their wake. I wanted more than anything to take this moment home with me as a souvenir, like one keeps a jar of sand or a pocket full of seashells. I'd set it proudly next to a framed photo of us smiling in the sunshine and look at it with fondness every time I passed by. But moments like this were fleeting and could not be kept in a bottle. So, I tucked my burning skin, my racing pulse, and my need to be loved deep inside. I buried it where no one else would ever find it—like a pirate's treasure—and wrote the map to it on my heart. Bits and pieces of Luke were buried all throughout me over the years, and this moment joined them like a wrecked ship coming to rest on the ocean floor.

As all good things must come to an end, the boat horn signaled for us to return. We gathered up our things, waved goodbye to our new porky friends, and headed back to the dock. The whole day was filled with beautiful experiences and scenery, but Luke's face lit up with joy was by far my favorite part. His warmth emanated through me, and by the time our ship docked back on Nassau, his sunshine had taken root inside my broken—yet healing—heart.

"Boy, you were Mr. Popular today with those pigs," I said, nudging him as we walked back to our room.

"Nah, they preferred you, I just kept gettin' in their way. Thank you for the fun day. Swimmin' in the ocean with livestock was an experience I never knew I needed."

He smiled and pushed me against the door, kissing my lips slowly one more time before we dipped away from public eyes.

As the door shut behind us, the tone of the day changed, and I didn't like it one bit. Luke began cautiously, "So, I feel like there's a lot we need to address, Stor. How about we go out back in that hammock and talk for a bit before dinner?"

My stomach looped around itself and as much as I didn't want to face reality, I knew we had to. We only had one more day here in Nassau, and there was a lot to figure out before we flew home. For one, where was home for me going to be? Would I go back to Little Creek and start fresh with Luke? Would I stay in Chicago and keep building my career? Would I need to find a job where I didn't have to see Dane every day, or could I handle seeing him around the office? There were far more question marks on my list than there were periods, and I wasn't sure which thing to tackle first.

"Sure, we can do that. Though I would much rather make out instead," I teased.

Luke laughed. "Yeah, that's not goin' to work on me, today. We gotta figure out the hard stuff first, then we can kiss some more," he promised, looking down at my lips.

I groaned. "Fine. But let the record show that my idea was more fun."

"Duly noted. And let the record also show that I agree with you, but avoidin' this is goin' to make things harder when we separate."

Separate. I hated that word all of a sudden. It was icky in my mouth like the word *moist* and I wanted to cast it far, far away from my vocabulary.

I dragged myself out to the patio and settled next to Luke in our awesome two-person hammock. Swaying gently in the breeze, I melted into him like butter on Ma Dixon's homemade biscuits.

"Okay, what did you want to talk about then?"

"First of all, I want you to know there's no pressure from me to quit your job and come home. Sure, ultimately, that's what I want because I want to build a life with you. But it needs to be *your* choice to come home, and no one else's."

I nodded. "You have always been so supportive of me, even at your own expense. Why is that? Why did you always sacrifice your own happiness for mine?"

"Because that's what love is to me, Stor. It gives me joy to put others before myself."

That statement hit me hard. I didn't know if I'd ever put his needs and wants first. I was accustomed to him being so agreeable that I never stopped to realize I was taking advantage of his love for me.

"I have been so unfair to you all these years."

"What do you mean?" His voice reverberated low in my ear on his chest.

"I don't think I have ever deserved one tiny bit of love you have given to me. I am by far the selfish one in this relationship, and I'm sorry."

He kissed the top of my head and chuckled softly. "Love isn't about deservin' Stor. It's about givin'. And it made me happy to give everything I had to you. Because that's what made *you* happy."

"Well, I have a lot of making up to do, that's all. You deserve a woman who gives as freely as you do."

"There you go again, using the word *deserve*. I have exactly what I need right here, and I'm content with that."

My heart sank into my stomach as my inadequacies bubbled to the surface.

"Why *do* you love me, Luke?"

He sighed and his chest moved up and down under my head. I could hear his heart beating and the unworthiness I felt to hold it in my hands screamed in my ears.

"Because lovin' you is like bein' on fire, and jumpin' out of an airplane, all at the same time. You make my heart race and my insides tumble with excitement. You know all my demons, all my secrets, and you still chose to be my best friend. I've never felt judged by you like I did from others in my life. I have never met another human I could be one hundred percent myself with and not be scared out of my wits about it."

"You have always been my safe harbor," I said quietly. "I wanted to tell you so many times what you meant to me. But I never could find the courage. I worried if I told you how I felt about you, that someday we'd fight and break up and I'd lose my first love and my best friend all in one shot. I couldn't imagine my life without you in it." I paused as the realization hit me: I had walked away from Luke to find myself and lost him anyway. "Then like a fool I cut you out on purpose."

Luke's hand paused from stroking my hair. "Why did you walk away from me like that? I don't think you'll ever understand how much that hurt me." The pain reverberated in his voice, though he tried his best to hide it.

I swallowed hard. I knew I'd have to give him an answer to that question one day. In all my years of searching for a good excuse as to why, I could never come up with one.

"Of all the things I regret in my life, that is the one that kills me most. I'm so sorry for how much I hurt you. I never meant to. I wanted so badly to erase who I was that I took down innocent bystanders with me. I think I believed that if I wanted to completely change myself, I needed to let go of everything and everyone that reminded me of the old Story. But the truth is, the further I got from the girl I tried to hide, the more I missed her. *And* you. Days turned into months, months turned into years, then it was too late. I'd burned bridges. I was ashamed of myself for turning my back on my best friend. After a while I convinced myself that you'd never forgive me, because *I* couldn't forgive myself for doing that to you. I knew I didn't deserve to have you in my life. So, I stayed gone."

"You never even gave me the chance to forgive you. You just made that choice for me."

"It sounds so black and white when you put it like that."

"It *is* black and white Stor. I would've forgiven you even if you were gone for longer than that. But I didn't know that's why you stopped talkin' to me. I thought you'd finally wised up to the fact that I wasn't enough for you, and that you had found some lucky college guy who was everything I wasn't. I had no choice but to let you go."

"So much for our stellar communication skills." I laughed and shook my head against his chest. "I wish I would've known you loved me all those years ago. Then maybe I would've stayed. Why did you keep your feelings from me?" I asked, tracing the buttons on his shirt.

"For precisely that reason. You would've stayed when you had dreams to chase." He raised a finger matter-of-factly. "In all fairness, though, I *did* tell you I loved you once."

I looked up sharply. "No, you didn't! I would've remembered that!"

He grinned. "I sure did. The night of your farewell party. Remember? I drove you home after you got too hammered to drive."

"I barfed on the floorboards of your truck."

"Yep. That's the one."

I shook my head in embarrassment. "I don't remember anything else from that night. You seriously told me you loved me?"

"I did. And then I panicked because for two seconds, right before you threw up, your eyes cleared and I thought you'd remember," he said with a laugh.

I slapped my forehead. "Not my finest moment."

"Maybe not. But it was a good memory to stash away."

"For whom? Me, you, or your truck?"

Luke laughed, causing the hammock to sway.

"Definitely for me. I'm not sure my truck fully recovered from it."

After a minute of silence, I asked, "So, what was your second thing?"

"Hmmm?"

"When we started this chat you said, 'first of all'. What was 'second of all' on your list to discuss?"

"Ah. Right. What do you think you're gonna do when you get back to Chicago? That is, if you are goin' back."

"Honestly, I'm not quite sure. I've avoided thinking about it, because I don't know what to do."

"Can you sign a new lease for your apartment?"

"No, I have to be out by the end of next month. The plan was just to move into Dane's place a little bit at a time, but now I've got to figure my stuff out quickly."

"You'll figure it out. And whatever you decide, I'm here to help you."

"I sure hope you're right. I want to just bury my head in the sand and ignore the impending doom of decisions coming. But apparently that's not a healthy coping mechanism," I joked. "Truth be told, that's a whole lot of uphill battles to fight, and I'm just not in the conquering mood."

"You will be. You'll get back to life and look at everything with fresh eyes, and I think your answers will become clearer."

I nodded, but inside I didn't feel so confident.

As our time together tipped toward the horizon like the sun at dusk, the panic to go back to my old life raged. I loved Luke, and after this trip I *knew* it like someone knows the streets of their hometown. Had he not stopped me from pushing our relationship too quickly, I would've gone all in—whether I was ready for it or not. It was then that it dawned on me that my marriage to Dane wouldn't have lasted. The pain from him dumping me faded like the flavor of cheap bubble gum, and the only lingering feelings came from unknowns and embarrassment.

Did I ever love Dane? Maybe. But not like I loved Luke. I kept pieces of myself back from Dane that love wouldn't have hidden. Pieces I never had to hide with Luke because he accepted all my imperfections. Dane pressured me to fit into a mold he wanted me in: an ideal I'd never meet but die trying. We were the power couple that everyone strived for and with that came a lot of pressure to be perfect. Deep down, I accepted his proposal because it was expected of us. The whole office placed bets on how long it took for Dane to put a ring on it. Back at home, people were impressed by his status. I had struck it rich, so it seemed only natural to get married. It never occurred to me that Luke loved me, so I took door number two and hoped for the best.

After "honeymooning" with Luke away from prying eyes, expectations, and pretenses, it was easy for me to let go of Dane. He wasn't real. His love wasn't real, and frankly, neither was mine. When I sloughed off the weight of forcing a relationship to work,

I realized how much pressure I was really under. My shoulders relaxed, I smiled more, I laughed from the depths of my soul, and I had hope that someday I could love again. And not just Luke, but also myself. Being under the thumb of someone that expected perfection from me fed a self-loathing I battled as long as I could remember. It reared its ugly head when I couldn't perform to his standards, and I was back in high school all over again. Letting go of the burden Dane placed on me healed my heart. It gave me the permission I needed to be happy with who I was, regardless of what others thought. And amid the turmoil of figuring my next step out, at least I had that to hang on to.

I had a long road ahead of me, but the courage to change sprouted toward the sunlight. *If I could only stay out of everyone's shadow...*

FOURTEEN

Luke

Our last day in Nassau we spent making out at the beach, which, honestly, was the perfect way to end the trip. It was also the only way I could distract myself from the storm of dread brewing inside. My fake honeymoon with Story set the bar really high for things I hoped would come, but an obnoxious thought overshadowed a good portion of our time, pestering my mind with a fear that this was a dream I'd eventually have to wake from. I wasn't sure when I'd see her again, so while I had the chance, I pulled her close to me as much as possible, trying to fill a tank that had a hole in the bottom.

When the morning came to catch flights, we both dragged our feet as long as we could. Although she never said she dreaded leaving out loud, her sad eyes, her slumped shoulders, and her forced smile did. I learned to read Story long ago, and as I looked at her in the security line at the airport, she was preoccupied with rough roads ahead.

I squeezed her hand, and she looked up at me with tears in her eyes. "Hey," I said, pulling her close. "No tears yet. We've still got sixteen hours worth of flights and layovers before we have to say goodbye."

"Yeah," she admitted with a shaky voice. "But I don't want to go back to reality. It's like the end of vacation blues, topped with the dread of going back to a life that looks more and more like a dumpster fire." She sighed heavily and leaned into my chest.

"If anyone can sift through all the mess and make somethin' beautiful out of it, it's you. Who knows? Maybe this is the best thing that could've happened to you in this phase of your life, 'cause it forced you out of your comfort zone and onto an unfamiliar path. But on that new path is where you'll grow and learn what really matters to you. Starin' all this in the face will make you stronger and more resilient, Stor. I believe that one hundred percent."

"I sure hope you're right, 'cause I feel like a disaster inside. When I look at everything that has fallen apart around me, it feels too overwhelming to sort out."

"Maybe what looks like everything fallin' apart, is really everything fallin' together," I said, wrapping my arms around her. "And remember, I'm only an eight-hour drive away. Anytime you need me, all you gotta do is call."

"Really?"

"Of course! I got a truck to haul stuff and a listenin' ear."

She sighed against my chest, and I felt her shoulders release some of the tension they were carrying.

"I'll always be here for you, Stor. I hope you know that."

"Yeah, I do. It's going to be hard to face some of this without you."

"Then don't. Call me anytime, I'll get the guys to take over my tasks on the farm and I'll be right there. Okay?"

Her chin quivered when she looked at me and replied a shaky, "Okay."

"Now, in the meantime, we need to hit the shops in here and get some more snacks for the plane. That piddly bag of peanuts they gave us on the flight over here did nothin' for me but make me hungrier."

I grabbed our carry-on bags and rolled them away from the security checkpoint while she shoved her shoes on and caught up.

THE PLANE RIDE TO MIAMI, the subsequent layover, and the flight to Chicago sapped us both dry. We leaned up against each other and slept a good portion of the flights and reminisced and laughed our guts out while we waited in the terminals.

But as we walked off the plane, Story turned on her phone and was inundated with messages and emails. She stopped mid-step and stared at her phone, scrolling and responding to massive amounts of requests for her time. I watched her face fall, then her whole demeanor changed. The air around her became thick, making me wade through rain and mud to get to her.

"This is my stop," she said with tears filling her eyes. "Your connecting flight to Omaha leaves in forty-five minutes, so we can't even hang out longer ..." she trailed off as she put her phone in her pocket.

"Maybe it's better this way. Rip off the bandage and get on with it before we have a chance to talk ourselves out of things," I replied weakly.

Heaven knew the last thing I wanted to do was walk away from Story, but it had to be done. She needed to face things in Chicago, and I wasn't necessarily a part of that unless she wanted me to be. So, this goodbye had to be as quick as possible. We both knew it would be completely unrealistic to expect it to be painless, so it was best just to take it head-on and let the chips fall where they may.

"I'm overwhelmed, Luke," she said as she wiped her eyes with a napkin from the plane. "I've built a good life here in Chicago. But then I think about rocking on porch swings and watching the sun go down over the cornfields, and I want that too."

I put my hands on her shoulders and squared up with her. The last time she left for Chicago, I didn't ask her to stay, and I regretted it every day afterward. I couldn't live with myself if I was dumb enough to make that mistake again. I gathered my courage, pushed the paralyzing fear that swarmed me down into my gut, and took my shot.

"This is somethin' you need to figure out for yourself, Stor. There isn't anybody who can make up your mind for you. But before I chicken out, I'm gonna plead my case with you."

"Choose me. Choose a simple life on a stretch of land you can be proud of. Have a bunch of babies with me and we'll raise 'em up right. Lay in my arms every night and we'll pillow-talk 'til dawn. Let's dance in the kitchen in our socks and go to tailgatin' parties when the 'Huskers are playin'.

"We can build a beautiful life full of joy and hard work and wrinkles around our eyes from years of laughter. Then when we're old and gray you can help me find my teeth and I'll help you up the porch steps. Yoke up with me, Stor," I pleaded, my voice shaking. Since I wasn't much of a crier I stopped talking.

Her face twisted in confusion, and I could see the difficulty in her eyes. When she opened her mouth to reply, I stopped her. I wasn't sure if it was because I was too scared of what she'd say back to me, or if I needed her to mull it over in the city before she made an informed choice. But whatever the reason, she didn't protest.

I pulled a small, perfectly white shell from my pocket and placed it into her palm, curling her fingers closed around it. "I found this on the beach that night I walked alone after the Newlywed Game. I want you to keep it to remember that even in the most difficult situations, you always have me, okay?"

She nodded as tears streamed down her face, and I was back in that courtyard on her wedding day, telling her to go marry Dane. It stung inside now, just like it did before. She gripped me like a lifeline and kissed my lips soft like butterfly wings.

"Thank you for coming with me. I needed you there more than you'll ever know." She paused and the look on her face made my heart sink like an anchor in my chest. "I've got a lot of decisions to make, and I need to get in a head space to think clearly. If you don't hear from me for a bit, that's why. I just need time to figure everything out."

I felt like I'd been slapped and had the wind knocked out of me all at the same time. She needed time to think, and I understood that. But I was hoping to be included a little more in her thought process. Would she disappear from my life again, just like before, even though she said she'd regretted it? I had hoped she would've taken me up on my offer and hopped on a plane to Omaha with me that instant instead of distancing herself from me again.

In self-preservation, I iced over.

"Well, you'd better get to it, then. I've got a plane to catch," I said as I adjusted my worn-out baseball cap and grabbed my suitcase. "I'll leave you to it." I forced a smile and pushed away the brokenness I felt inside. "Bye, Stor."

I walked away. I left her standing there in the airport with tears in her eyes and defeat on her face.

I was tempted more than once to turn around and look back at her, but my heart couldn't take it if she wasn't doing the same. It was the hardest thing to leave with so much uncertainty between us, but she needed to make decisions on her own. I prayed with my whole heart that in the end she'd choose me and come home. However, in that moment, a tiny seed of doubt that she would, in fact, choose me, sprouted to the surface in my heart.

I was worried.

FIFTEEN

Story

Luke left me. I reacted like a coward when he asked me to come home and build a beautiful life with him, and I hesitated just long enough to instill doubt in both of us. *What have I done?* I fought the urge to run after him, to wrap my arms around his neck and confess that he had always been the one who held my heart. I wanted to throw caution to the wind and hop on the plane to Omaha. I wanted to shout over the crowd that I loved him and always would. But I stood frozen in place, watching Luke get smaller and smaller as he disappeared from view. People buzzed all around me, yet I had never felt more alone in my entire life than I did in that terminal, clutching the shell Luke left in my hand.

The ride home to my dark apartment matched the dismal rainy weather outside, and my tears fell like the raindrops down the window of the car. Weary from traveling, I dropped everything right at the door, sank into a bubble bath, and bawled my eyes out. The whole idea of what to do next overpowered me, so I forced myself to lay down and sleep. I had two days to pull myself together before I had to be back at the office. I'd use them to figure out what I wanted most ... and probably take some much-needed aggression out on some of Dane's belongings he left at my place.

———

By Monday, everyone either had a pitiful look or sympathetic pat on the back ready for me. It bordered on annoying because I walked into the office with as much strength as I could muster. I wanted to focus solely on my job, survive the day, then go back home. But every person I encountered brought it all up to the surface again. Like ripping a fresh scab from a wound repeatedly, by lunchtime I was exhausted.

"Girl! You didn't even warn me about what happened at your wedding!" Olivia hissed as she shut my office door behind her. "Are you okay?"

"No, not really," I said with a shaky voice. "But I will figure things out, I suppose."

"When Dane showed up here without you—or a ring—while you were supposed to be on your honeymoon, I sent you a million texts!"

"Yeah, my phone has basically been turned off since he left me at the altar. Sorry for not answering."

"I get it, but now you need to spill the tea. Let's go down to O'Malley's for lunch and you can tell me all about it." She looped her arm around mine and led me out the door.

I glanced around the pub, which was unusually empty for the lunch hour, and chose a spot next to the pool tables. After the waiter took our order, Olivia put her hand on mine.

"Okay, now tell me all about it," she said with a sympathetic smile.

I reiterated the whole series of events from finding Luke's love letter, to being left at the altar, and the subsequent "honeymoon" with Luke. Olivia's eyes grew wide and stayed that way.

"Girl, you've been through the wringer! I cannot believe all of that happened. And of course, I couldn't be there with you to be a shoulder to cry on. I totally would've gone to Nassau with you, but it sounds to me like Luke was the better option anyway." She winked. "So, what's next?"

"That, I'm not sure of. Part of me wants to stay, and part of me wants to go be with Luke in Little Creek."

"What's keeping you here? Besides me and all my fabulousness, of course." She grinned and flipped her hair over her shoulder dramatically.

"You're a big reason, that's true. And, I worked hard for this job. I'm not sure I can just walk away from it."

"You are extremely valuable at Wallace and Chambers, but a job isn't enough of a reason to stay if your heart is elsewhere. Jobs come and go, but finding true love with your best friend is priceless."

"You're not mad at me for considering going back home?"

"I'll be sad to see you go. But our friendship can withstand a few hundred miles of distance. We will just have to meet for girls' weekends instead of going to lunch every day."

"You make it sound so easy."

"I'm a hopeless romantic, I'll always choose love." She raised her eyebrows. "I have an idea," she said, grabbing two straw wrappers. She wrote a "C" on one, and an "L" on the other. "This wrapper means you choose Chicago. This wrapper means you choose Luke."

She poked them up through her fingers, but held them in her hand so I couldn't tell which was which.

"Now, pick one, but don't pull it out. Just tap on it."

I studied the slips of paper like my life depended on it, then tapped the one on the right.

"This one."

"Okay, now before I tell you which one you chose, which do you *hope* that it is?"

I shook my head. "What do you mean?"

"In your heart of hearts, you're hoping that it's one over the other. Which do you hope it is?"

My eyes stung and I blinked away the tears that formed. My hands absent-mindedly twisted at the napkin on the table, and I sighed.

"I would've picked Luke too," she said softly. "Your eyes shine when you talk about him."

I forced a smile and touched her hand on the table. "Yeah. He's incredible. I hope you get to meet him someday."

"Moment of truth: do you want to know which wrapper you actually chose?"

I shook my head. "No. This by itself was enough to help me make up my mind. Thank you."

She smiled. "Of course. But I've got to know." She opened her hand and peeked at which slip I had chosen.

"Now I'm curious. Which was it?"

"I'll never tell."

The waiter brought the check, and she snatched it up before I could.

"I'm keeping this secret from you, but to make it up to you, I'll buy your lunch."

I nodded. "Deal."

We gathered up our purses and jackets and stood to leave. As she set them on the table, I glanced down long enough to see I had chosen Chicago.

I breathed a sigh of relief and hugged her.

"You will never know how much I love you," I said quietly.

"I love you right back."

AFTER I RETURNED from lunch with Olivia, my secretary rapped on my door frame and waited until I looked up from my computer before coming in.

"Mr. Wallace would like to see you this afternoon," she said in her whiney voice. It sounded extra nasally today.

I struggled to like her as a person, but as a secretary she was top-notch. I dealt with her irritating voice because it meant I got to keep her organizational skills.

"Did he say what it pertained to?" My reply didn't come out as calm as I would've liked it to, and I hated the way I sounded.

"Nope. Just that he wanted you in his office when you had a sec," she replied, then walked out the open door.

"Great," I whispered to myself. I swigged a giant gulp of water to wet my dry throat and headed down the hall.

Mr. Wallace's office was at the end of the hallway, in a corner that was nothing but windows. That's what the CFO of a large accounting firm got: a huge corner office and a seven-figure salary.

I stepped into his office, and he signaled for me to sit down while he finished up his phone call. I stared out the window and watched the low-hanging clouds wander by, wondering if I was about to get canned.

After he hung up the phone, he put both sausage-like hands on the desk and cleared his throat. "I hear the wedding didn't go the way it should've, and I'm sorry for that," he said with very little sympathy in his eyes.

I had to pull every ounce of courage I had together to keep myself from tearing up. *I was an island. Nothing affected me. I would not cry in my boss' office.*

"I wanted to check in with you. See how you're getting on," he said, waving a lazy hand.

"I'm doing okay," I managed to squeak out.

Before I could continue, he interrupted, "And I also wanted to make sure you understand my expectations, Astoria," he said sternly, locking his hands in front of him. "This is not high school. I don't want any drama here, and if you don't think you can work alongside Dane anymore, say so now. I pride myself in the professionalism of our company, and that expectation still stands, even if you were dumped at the altar."

His words stunned me into silence. Had he always been so cold and unfeeling? I had never noticed it before, but now that I needed sympathy, I realized how cutthroat Mr. Wallace was. I managed to stammer through something to satisfy him and stood on shaking legs to leave.

"Astoria?" he said. "My daughter Daphne is coming in for a meeting today at two o'clock. You can go home early and work remotely if you'd like. She has requested you not be here when she comes in."

His *daughter* Daphne. *Holy crap!* The Daphne that broke up my wedding was Mr. Wallace's daughter? How had I not known? Had I seen her around and not noticed her before?

My mind reeled. Not only did I feel like my life was a huge mess, but now I worried I would lose my job too. She could insist her daddy dearest fire me, and I'd bet he'd do it.

I walked back to my office feeling like I had a target on my back and gathered up my laptop. I threw everything I needed in my bag and high-tailed it to my car. The last thing I needed was to see Dane and Daphne together after I had managed to avoid running into him all day.

I cried the whole way home, and by the time I padlocked my door shut, my sorrow had turned to anger. I ripped the photographs of me and Dane off the walls, tore him out of them and threw his pieces in the trash. I gathered his toothbrush and cologne from my medicine cabinet and tossed them too. I pulled his weekend changes of clothes from my closet, his fancy coffee machine that I never used, and every other thing in the apartment that reminded me of him and put it all in a big garbage bag.

I dragged that bag down to my car and heaved it into my trunk. Tomorrow, I would leave it next to his car, and he could do with it what he wanted.

The bare walls and end tables stared back at me without their usual photographs on display, but I felt so much better to not have reminders of him everywhere. Then I took that shell from my pocket and placed it where my old engagement photo sat on my nightstand. That way I'd see it every day to remind me that Luke cared. He always had.

SIXTEEN

Story

Two Years Ago

I walk off the elevator at work with a bit of pep in my step. I have an appointment at Hansen Foods to wow them into hiring our firm for their financial handling. They are the largest food processing plant in the Midwest. And although their farms are mainly in Nebraska and Iowa, their headquarters are right here in Chicago.

We've been schmoozing their executives for weeks, and now it's time to visit where it all began: their largest farm. My Mecca. My turf. I'm so confident in my ability to speak "farm girl" that when Mr. Wallace asked for a volunteer from accounting to escort our top financial executive, Dane Michaels, to their Omaha farm, I jumped at the chance. Plus, if everything goes according to plan, I will get the partnership with Dane I've been vying for.

Dane and I have been secretly dating for over six months, and stealing secret glances and meeting in supply closets for a quick kiss is getting old. I can hardly contain myself with the chance to spend two whole days with him out of the prying eyes of the office.

I roll my suitcase through the long tile corridors on the twenty-

fifth floor of our office building. My heels click softly on the floor, accompanied by the whirring sound of the wheels on my suitcase. I wait for Dane to arrive with his own luggage before I ask my secretary to call the car for us.

The company car drops us off at the airport, and at last I have two uninterrupted days with Dane all to myself. While I can hardly hide my grin, his poker face reveals nothing about his feelings about this business trip together. He's so good about hiding his affections for me at the office, that sometimes I wonder if the flowery things he says to me over the weekends are real.

After the company car drives away at the terminal drop-off, I turn excitedly toward him and grab his hand. His face relaxes a bit, and he smiles.

"Can I tell you how thrilled I am to spend two whole days with you in the middle of the week?" I gush. "We never get weekday time together outside the office."

"I know, it'll be great. But we still can't let on that we are dating—especially in front of our potential clients. If they get wind that we are anything but professional, we could lose this deal. Mr. Wallace will lose faith in my ability to land high-priced clients, and I won't get the big accounts anymore. Let's just keep things platonic looking unless we are alone, okay?"

I sigh. Of course, I don't expect to hold hands or kiss in front of the people at Hansen Foods, but the fact that he still wants to hide our relationship, even eight hours away from Chicago, is a bit disheartening. I pride myself in being professional, and that's what I'll be. Come hell or high water, I will succeed in my career. Even if that means my love life is less-than stellar.

"Yeah, okay," I agree glumly. "But will we get to have a nice dinner out, just the two of us?"

"Maybe. Unless the big wigs want to take us to dinner. We need to be one hundred percent available. We can't make any fancy reservations ahead of time."

My lovely ideas of romantic dinners at a rooftop restaurant in

Omaha or a lively night at a popular local brewery fade. Dane has said he loves me plenty of times. But he doesn't seem proud to be with me, and that's unsettling.

My dad still watches my mom walk into a room with a look on his face that says, "Man, I'm lucky she's mine," and I want so badly for a man to look at me that way too.

But Dane is too much business to worry about matters of the heart most of the time. Occasionally he'll do something super sweet for me that usually makes up for the time between his gestures. But I'm realizing on this trip that he may never look at me the way my dad looks at my mom. And I have to learn to be okay with that if I'm going to continue to pursue this relationship.

We check *into our hotel rooms and head up the elevator with our luggage.*

"I need to change really quick," I say as I unlock my door.

Dane checks his watch. "Well, hurry. We have an appointment, and I don't want to be late. We don't have time to waste."

"I know, I'll be fast, I promise," I reply through the crack in the door then let it swing shut behind me.

Ten minutes later, I walk out into the hallway in my jeans and boots.

Dane looks me up and down and snickers. "What on Earth are you wearing, Astoria? This is a business meeting, not a hoe-down."

"If I'm visiting a farm, I'd better be ready to walk through manure," I say with a confident smile. Although on the inside I suddenly doubt myself.

"Whatever you say. You don't have time to change now, so let's get going," he says, grabbing my hand.

His touch is reassuring, even if his words are not. And that's the epitome of our relationship: Give me the right amount of affection to keep me coming back, but with the undertone that I may never be enough for him. And because I want so desperately to show everyone back at home that I can be successful, I accept his breadcrumbs and dive further into my job to feel validation.

He kisses me in the elevator, but only because we're alone. The moment the doors slide open in the lobby, he steps away, drops my hand, and we're all business again. I'm not sure why I'm continually disappointed by Dane's actions toward me. That's just him. And who am I to ask a penguin to be anything but a penguin?

He stops the car on the gravel parking lot at an enormous farm, and a cloud of dust settles around my feet as I get out. I inhale deeply and sigh with contentment. It has been so long since I've smelled farm life, I didn't realize I had missed it so much.

Dane, on the other hand, frowns when the scent of livestock and dirt hits his delicate, city-boy nose, and I laugh out loud. He smiles, less-than amused, and buttons his suit jacket as a man in a Stetson approaches.

"You must be Astoria and Dane from Wallace and Chambers. I'm John Hansen, owner of Hansen Foods, and head of operations. The rest of the crew is out working. If you'd like to take a tour of the farm, we can introduce you as we come across 'em."

"Sounds great," I say, shaking his hand. He has the grip of a hardworking man, strong and calloused, and it makes me miss Luke. "It's so nice to be here, Mr. Hansen."

"Ah, call me John. My father was Mr. Hansen, and I doubt I'll answer if you call me that again," he says, laughing.

"John it is, then."

Dane sticks out his freshly manicured hand and shakes John's. I see a slight grimace on Dane's face at John's grip. Out here in the Midwest, when a man shakes another man's hand, he does so with purpose. Dane is used to power suits and high rollers who shake hands to establish dominance or instill intimidation. But John is the type who means what he says and keeps his word. And his handshake reflects that.

John looks Dane up and down and smiles politely. "You'll have to watch your step around here, son. Those fancy shoes'll get ruined real fast if you're not careful." He turns to me and grins. "Now you, Astoria, seem to know your way around the farm. Those boots look nice and broken in!"

"You betcha, sir, but call me Story, everyone back home does. I was born and raised in Little Creek, about forty-five miles from here. My folks grow soybeans and corn and have a few cows and some chickens to eat from."

"Well, that's just fine. I'm glad to see the big dogs at corporate sent me a Nebraska girl to make deals with. I'm feeling better 'bout this already. Now, if you tell me you're a 'Husker fan, I may seal the deal right now."

I reply with enthusiasm, "Go Big Red!" and have him eating from my hands faster than a football snap.

He laughs a loud, boisterous laugh and says, "Come on, now. I'll show you two around."

I look over my shoulder at Dane as we walk away, and I can't quite read his stony expression. Is it jealousy? I'm not quite sure. But whatever is going through his mind gives me the vindication I need to take the driver's seat and put the pedal to the metal.

***

THE TOUR around the farm takes about two hours. John shows us every part of the business, from the heavy equipment to the animals themselves. I'm in heaven as we wander, and when we're finished, I don't want to leave.

"The missus would like to have you both over for supper tonight if you don't mind. She's been preppin' for days to feed you her famous chicken pot pie, freshly baked biscuits, and she makes the best puppy chow in town! I'll make sure she has a fresh bowl when you come tonight."

For half a second, Dane's face shows panic.

I lean over and whisper in his ear, "'Puppy chow' isn't dog food.

It's what everyone else calls, Muddy Buddies. It's the treat made with Chex, peanut butter, chocolate, and powdered sugar."

The panic fades into relief and I wish I had let him sweat it out a bit more before offering an explanation. *He'll struggle with supper tonight, so I'll go easy on him.* He hates eating at places where he can't read the reviews or verify the cleanliness scores of the kitchen. *I, on the other hand, am hankering for a home-cooked meal and gladly accept for the both of us.*

John waves from the gate as we ease through. "See you tonight!" he yells over the tires spinning on the gravel road.

As soon as we pull away, Dane turns to me and frowns. "Astoria, I am a bit surprised at your unprofessionalism today. This is a big deal for the firm. Why were you so casual?"

"Because that's how we do things around here, Dane. Money doesn't impress men like John, hard work does. Helping him with the animals and hauling feed bags was my way of showing him that we will work hard for him."

"Oh, I see. So, you played the farm girl card so he would think we were one of them. Smart."

"I am 'one of them,' Dane. You forget that I grew up on a farm too. All my neighbors were farmers or ranchers, and most of my friends worked on their family's land."

"Huh. Well, I'm glad you came along then," he says, patting my knee. "I'm gonna need the hotel to dry clean this suit and shine my shoes tonight." He dusts the dirt from his pant legs.

I shake my head. "Did you at least bring a pair of jeans you can wear tomorrow? You stuck out like a sore thumb walking around a farm in a suit," I say, giggling.

"Well, no. I had no intention of dressing casually on this trip."

"Then let's go get you some before we head back for supper. I know you hate dressing down, but you'll put the Hansens at ease if you relax a little."

"I guess, if you say so ..." he trails off.

"I do. And it'll be fine."

MRS. HANSEN's home smells of fresh-baked biscuits from a recipe that's most likely generational, and the aroma of chicken pot pie hits me like a wrecking ball when we enter the kitchen. My mouth waters and I make a mental note to ask her for her recipes later. I have to restrain myself from sitting down at the table and squealing with delight, because I feel like Winnie the Pooh about to get a pot of honey. There's nothing like fresh, homemade cooking, and I am here. For. It.

Dane glances around the kitchen, and when his face relaxes, I know he's satisfied with the cleanliness of it. I nudge his ribs and tell him he has no reason to worry.

"Astoria, I'm sitting in a successful man's home in blue jeans, about to eat dinner at his kitchen table. Not even a dining room table. We are literally in the kitchen. I'm feeling a bit out of my element here," he whispers.

"Well, not to worry. This is pretty standard practice. You'd fit in better if you'd just un-pinch your face."

"My face is pinched?"

"Yes. And it has been since you stepped in manure this morning. Relax, please. The Hansens are good people, and they want to make you feel at home."

"Well, this isn't exactly my version of 'home,' but I'll do my best to 'un-pinch' my face," he says, chuckling.

Eventually, his shoulders release the tension he's holding, and the lines in his forehead disappear. He even laughs a few times at dinner. And when Mrs. Hansen explains that most of her ingredients are fresh from either her land or a neighbor's, Dane looks genuinely impressed.

It's the best meal I've had in a long time, and I tell her so. She stuffs a goody bag full of puppy chow for us to take back to the hotel. I'm not even ashamed to admit that it doesn't last longer than the car ride home. My lap is covered in powdered sugar when I step out of the car, so I covertly brush off the evidence as best as I can.

By the time we leave for the airport at the end of our trip, John has all but signed papers to hire the firm. Hansen Foods will be one of our top accounts, and I helped land them. Me. A small-town country girl who knows her way around a farm and a farmer. I ride home with a smile so big my cheeks hurt. I can't wait to see Mr. Wallace's face when he finds out what an asset I am.

SEVENTEEN

Luke

I wrestled with frustration on my flight home from Chicago. The way we left things made me unsettled inside, and I worried Story would slip through my fingers again. *Had I done enough to show her how much she meant to me? Would she make it back to work and realize our time together was a mistake?* This all too familiar panic sat heavy on my shoulders, and I dreaded going back to regular, everyday life. A giant hole replaced the heart in my chest, and I had to go about the rest of my night like I wasn't gaping open.

Pa Dixon picked me up at the airport and drove extra slow once we hit the gravel roads near home.

"You've been awfully quiet, son. Y'okay?" he asked me in his rough old voice.

"Yeah, I'm fine Pa. I just ..."

"Miss her already, huh?"

"The second I walked away from her in Chicago I missed her. And I'm not sure how to reconcile that feelin'."

"Oh, completely understand. When I left your grandma behind to go fight in Korea, it was like I left half of me back home. Functioning without her by my side for so long felt foreign to me. I carried her photo in my pocket and wrote to her every day," he said smiling. A reminiscent gleam formed in his eyes, and although he was next to me in his old beat-up truck, he looked far away in his youth, courtin' the most beautiful girl he'd ever seen.

"I want that," I said quietly.

"You want what, son?"

"That. A love so strong it carried you through hell. A connection so deep you weren't satisfied unless you wrote to her about your day. And a friendship so lastin' it didn't matter how long you were apart, you picked up right where you left off when you came back home."

"You have that with Story, too."

"Maybe. When we're together, I think we do. Especially in Nassau. We reached a whole new level in our relationship. But the second her feet hit the ground in Chicago, everything changed. She became unsure of herself, questioned what she wanted, and then pushed me away. It was so weird."

"Well, she's got a lot of things to think about. It's all big, life-alterin' decisions. Give her time, Luke. She'll come 'round. Be the rock she needs to crumble against when she falls apart, and she'll understand what choice to make."

"Yeah, I know. I'm just sick of waitin'."

"I get that. But true love like what you two have is worth the wait. The only thing you can do now is make sure you're the best man for the job. So, when she comes back, you're ready to offer up the finest version of yourself to her."

I nodded. Pa was right. He was *always* right. "Thank you. I needed some wisdom tonight," I said, patting his shoulder as we pulled into my driveway.

"Anytime, son. Anytime," he replied, tipping his hat at me. "Do you need some help getting your bags inside?"

"Nah. They're not too heavy. You go on home to Ma. I'll see you in the mornin'. Thanks for the ride."

"Of course. You're welcome to come for breakfast if you'd

like. Otherwise, I'll see you in the fields!" he hollered out the open window as he backed up.

I stood on the porch and waved until he disappeared into a cloud of dust, then stepped into a dark, lonely house.

Five Years Ago

MY OLD TRUCK *bumps along on the gravel road out to the new plot of land I'd signed on the day prior. Story sits shotgun, the wind blowing through her hair as her hand rides the wind out the window. She has a relaxed smile, and although she's only home for a rare week visit, and I barely heard from her while she was away, we've fallen right back into our regular pattern.*

"I can't wait for you to see it," I say grinning. "It's perfect. It has a small creek runnin' through it, plenty of room for a barn and a few animals, and nice mature trees shadin' where the backyard will be."

"I'm so happy for you, Lukie. Look at you, chasing your dreams and catching them."

"Well, I could just as easily say the same about you, Miss Head of Accounting at Wallace and Chambers."

"Isn't it great? I've worked so hard for this. So many late nights and missed celebrations, and it finally paid off."

We pull onto a rough gravel road, and I slow to a stop then kill the engine. "Here it is! My own piece of the world. And the coolest part is, I get to name the street and everything, since it's on a private lane."

"What are you going to call it?" she asks, slamming the truck door behind her.

"I'm not sure yet. Somethin' nice, like Sunset Lane or Windmill Way."

Story smiles and I see the wheels turning in her pretty little head. I drop the tailgate down on the back of the truck and we hop up into our old spots. I grab a couple of sodas from the Styrofoam cooler in the bed of the truck and hand one to her. She sighs contentedly, swinging her feet back and forth and takes in my land.

"This is a beautiful place to put down some roots, Lukie. I can see it now: A cute little farmhouse over there," she says, pointing toward the long grasses, "a big red barn out back, and rows of corn that seem to stretch on forever. If you built the house there"—she points—"you could have shade on your back porch every evening. With the house facing west, you could put a couple of rocking chairs on the front porch and watch the sun go down."

"Now that sounds like a great plan," I reply with a sigh. "Hey. I have an idea. How 'bout you come with me to meet with the builder tomorrow so you can help pick a house plan."

"Oh, I couldn't possibly. This is your thing. You should have your house exactly how you like it."

"I know, but it'd be nice to have a woman's perspective. I'm no good at thinkin' about practical things like facin' the sunset at night and how to choose paint colors and tile and such. Will you please come help me?" I beg.

"If you insist. But I want you to have what you want. I am only there to give a woman's perspective. Okay?"

"Deal."

I take a swig of my soda to hide my smile. In all reality, I want her to pick as much of that house as I can talk her into choosing, because in the back of my mind, I want her to grow old with me in it. And on days when she's back in the city, I want to be reminded of her when I run my hand down the banister she chose or brush my teeth in the bathroom she picked out. That way, I'll always have a little piece of her with me, even if she's gone.

"Porch Swing Lane," she says, breaking my train of thought.

"Huh?" I say with confusion in my tone.

"That's what you should name your street."

"Porch Swing Lane. I like it," I say, mulling it over in my

mind. "But if I name it that, I definitely gotta have a porch swing to sit on."

"Exactly. Isn't it cute? It has such a country feel to it."

"I love it," I reply. The embers in my heart burn more brightly at the thought of it. And her. "It's perfect."

EIGHTEEN

Story

I fought my way through my first week back in Chicago. After Mr. Wallace sent me home on Monday I tried to blend into the walls when I worked in the office. Heaven knows I had plenty of practice growing up on how to be unseen in public. I was a masterful wallflower at heart, and I dug deep inside to channel that shy, nerdy girl I'd spent so many years covering up.

Every day at two o'clock I'd close my laptop, shut my office door, and sneak out. Working the rest of the day from home helped me be more productive anyway. It drained me to work in the office where people whispered about me until I approached, followed by fake sympathetic smiles. I ran into Dane a few times by accident, and although the awkwardness flashed like a neon sign in front of us, the heartache I had expected to accompany seeing him was somehow absent. I didn't want to kick and scream and make a scene. I wanted to cease to exist in his world. Or, rather, I didn't want him to exist in mine.

I had taken the garbage bag of all his things and plunked it next to his trunk on Tuesday. But even after ridding my house of his things, my work life was still very much intertwined with him. And I hated it.

Friday morning when I opened my office door, I found a bright orange sticky note on my desk. Dane was the only one in the office who used the orange ones, so I knew right away that the note was from him. I hung my cardigan up by the door and flopped my laptop bag onto my chair, glancing down at the note while I unpacked. I shook my head as I read it.

> *Astoria,*
> *Please come by my office today when you can. We need to*
> *talk.*
> *-D*

He signed it just like old times, but there was nothing between us like old times. We were not on a nickname basis anymore, and I scoffed at the audacity he had to assume we could be. I crumpled it up and tossed it in my trash can.

I shot a quick text to Olivia.

Story: Dane asked me to come to his office. (wide-eyed emoji.)

Olivia: No way! Are you going to oblige?

Story: I wish I could, but I don't want to.

THEN I SENT a gif with the *Friends* reference.

Olivia: Should I run defense for you in case he comes your way?

Story: Nah. I've got to see him eventually
anyway. But if I text you 9-1-1, send in recon.

IT WASN'T an hour later that he knocked lightly, ripping me
from the spreadsheet I was knee-deep in.

He hovered in the doorway like a balloon losing its helium
and cleared his throat. "Did you get my note?"

"Yep." I motioned to the trash can. "I filed it with all of my
important papers."

"Funny," he said, rolling his eyes.

"What do you need, Dane? I'm kinda busy."

"I came to talk about Hansen Foods. I talked to them while
you were gone, and I need you to see my notes."

"So, you schmoozed up to my best client while I was out of
the country, on our honeymoon without you? That doesn't
sound at all suspicious."

"I just wanted to keep the dialogue between them open."

"That was my role."

"Well, maybe if you'd at least *talk* to me, I could've clued you
in before now. You used to spend half your workday in my office.
Now I rarely see you all week long."

"That's on purpose."

"Come on, don't be a child about this."

I almost forgot how condescending he could be. *Almost.*

I scoffed. "Really, Dane? My avoiding you is childish? You
embarrassed me in front of our family and friends, up ended my
whole life, my plans, my future, and I am expected to come into
work every day and act completely normal?

"I am doing the very best I can, only to have your budding
relationship with the *boss' daughter* thrown in my face every time I
turn around. I'm the subject of office gossip, and because I want
to give people less to talk about, I'm being *childish*? You're not the
one who has to endure the whispering of your co-workers or the
fact that everyone goes silent when you enter a room now.

"You don't think I see their shifty eyes watching every move I make, wondering if I'm going to lose it any moment? I am being as much of an adult about all of this as I can possibly muster, so don't you *dare* judge me for the way I'm coping," my voice rose, and I noticed I was drawing the attention of those trickling in, so I zipped my mouth shut.

"For Pete's sake, you're making a scene. This is not the time or place to air our dirty laundry."

"You're right. It's not," I said, gathering up what was left of my dignity and slid my chair over to make room for him at my desk. "Make it quick."

He closed the door and sighed heavily. "I'm sorry, I shouldn't have said you were childish. I know this is hard for you, and I'm sorry for that too. If it's worth anything, you look good."

He scooted his chair too close to me, and my brain raised a red flag.

"You don't get to say that to me anymore, Dane," I said flatly. "Our relationship is strictly business now."

"Astoria," he argued.

"You wanted to talk about Hansen Foods?"

"You can't avoid me forever. You leave a garbage bag full of my stuff at my car, you take the long way to the bathroom so you don't have to pass my office, and I haven't seen you get coffee at all. What gives?"

I laughed and shook my head. "Did you come in here with the prospect of talking about our client, only to bait and switch me once I invited you in?

"The truth is you walked away from me. You exchanged our plans for someone else. You are no longer a player on the field in my life. You are a spectator in the nosebleeds who has to watch everything I do with a pair of binoculars.

"So, you don't get to be hurt by the fact that I avoid you at all costs and make a new routine that doesn't include you. You removed yourself from the equation, Dane. I'm just filling in the holes now." I stood and opened my office door. "We are done here. If you have any questions about Hansen Foods, email me."

"Astoria— "

Before he could even finish his sentence, I held up my hand to stop him. "I'm done, Dane."

An insulted expression crossed his face, and I wondered if that was the first time in his life that a woman had actually shut him down. He stood slowly and walked toward the hallway.

"You're making a big mistake."

"Nope. I'm pretty sure I avoided one. I owe you thanks for that at least," I said, slapping him on the back.

Olivia glanced up from her computer and mouthed, "Are you okay?"

I nodded and blinked away my tears before shutting my office door.

THAT EVENING I wandered restlessly around my apartment like a ghost with nothing to haunt. The confrontation at the office numbed me to my bones and sucked the life out of me. I was so tired of living in limbo. Like my future was in someone else's hands, and that was definitely not where I wanted to be.

I dragged out my laptop and started the search for a new job, and new apartment, possibly closer to Omaha, but nothing grabbed me. Discouraged, I slammed the lid shut and began packing up a moving box. I may not have a clear path for what is next, but I knew I couldn't stay where I was.

Stupid Dane. Stupid Daphne. Stupid change of heart. Everything had been upended. Yet, I had myself to blame as much as them. Had Daphne not stood up, *I* would have been the one leaving *Dane* at the altar. Either way, one of us got our heart broken. Deep down I was grateful that Dane had been the one to pull the trigger, even if it hurt, because I got to keep the status of the heroine in my story intact. I shook my head at the idea of us going through with the wedding. I'd rather have this mess over what would've been, that's for sure. *Bullet. Dodged.*

I sat cross-legged in the middle of my bedroom floor and pulled a bin of old photographs from under my bed. I flipped through years of silly pretend photo shoots Liz and I did in ridiculous outfits with heavily applied makeup. Liz was sure that she'd be famous someday. I, on the other hand, never craved the spotlight. The more I blended in at life, the better.

I snapped a photo and shared it in a text message to Liz and set the photos aside.

The stack of pictures with me and Luke tripled the size of the one with Liz, and I had to keep it wrapped with a big, fat, rubber band. My heart ached for those carefree days of riding around in his truck, jumping off the bridge into the river, and campfires with s'mores. But our senior prom photo was by far my favorite.

We couldn't stop laughing at the cheesy pose the photographer put us in, so our photo was beautifully candid of us cracking up. It was the very definition of our relationship: easy, fun, and joyful. We were posed like lovers but laughing like friends. It was perfection, and looking at that photo took me right back to that night.

Senior Prom

LUKE and I spend every beautiful day after school at our old "thinking spot" by the creek. So much so that we each have a picnic blanket in our cars so we don't have to sit on the ground. Only a select few even know where it is, and no one else is allowed to come. It's our little corner of heaven where we can be real and vulnerable and laugh until our faces hurt.

"Are you really not going to go?" I ask Luke, frowning.

"Nah. Jenna's brother graduates from boot camp this weekend,

and her parents are making her go to it. So even if I wanted to go to prom, I don't have a date," he replies, picking the grass beside his legs and letting it blow away.

"That's dumb."

"Why is it dumb?"

"Because it's our senior prom! You should be going!" I protest.

"I don't care about that near as much as you do, Stor. You know that. The only way I'd go now is if I could take you. And Josh already beat me to it."

I fold my arms. Josh isn't my first choice for a date, but Luke has a girlfriend, and she has first dibs on him, which I totally hate. Had I known she was going to ditch out last minute, I wouldn't have committed to going with anyone. I sigh, pick a dandelion, and make a wish.

I wish Luke was taking me to prom tonight.

I DO the finishing touches on my makeup as my mom finishes curling my hair. My soft brown waves hang down my back, and a tiny flower crown weaves into a braid that circles the top of my head.

"You are so beautiful," my mom says with a smile. "Josh is going to love how you look tonight."

"Yeah," I say, trying hard to hide my disappointment.

My mom checks her watch. "What time did he say we would be here again?"

"Five thirty," I reply, checking my phone. It's six o'clock. Thirty minutes late is no big deal. Plus, I just finished getting ready, so it's good that he's running behind.

"Maybe he's on his way. Did he call?"

"No. And the last time I called; he didn't answer his phone. I'll try texting him and see where he is."

"Okay, sweet girl. I'll be downstairs if you need help getting zipped up."

"Thanks, mama," I say as I pick up my phone.

Six thirty rolls around, and still no word from Josh. When he asked me a few weeks ago to be his date, my brain threw a flag on the play. It seemed too good to be true, but the desire to go to prom at all trumped any logic that he may be doing it as a joke. Now I know. I want to beat myself up for being so naive. I fight back tears of embarrassment at being stood up on prom night and wonder how long it will take until everyone else at school will know. But after wallowing in self-pity for a few minutes, I zip up my bright yellow dress, grab my keys, and head downstairs.

"*I'm going to go to Luke's. If Josh shows up, tell him he missed his chance,*" *I say over my shoulder to my parents as I walk out the front door.*

My heels sink in the grass at Ma and Pa Dixon's house as I cross the yard. I should've worn my boots, they're way more comfortable and practical. *I decide to kick my shoes off and carry them in my hands the rest of the way instead. My heart pounds as I take the steps up the porch and raise my hand to knock.* Why am I so nervous right now? It's just Luke. *But who am I kidding? It hasn't been "just Luke" for quite some time. I take a deep breath and knock my secret way that I only do for him. There's a shuffling inside, then the door swings open.*

"*Oh, Story, you look absolutely stunning my dear! I've hardly ever seen you without your glasses on. I like it!*" *Ma says as she cups my face in her hands and smiles wide.* "*Come on in, sweetheart.*" *She hollers up the stairs,* "*Luke! You have a visitor!*"

Luke rounds the upstairs corner in his usual trying-to-break-his-last-record speed, but stops like he hit a wall when he sees me in the foyer. He stands frozen at the top of the stairs, gripping the banister. He swallows hard, and his lips part slightly as he exhales. His eyes study me from bare feet to braided crown before he clutches his chest with an open hand and smiles.

"*Wow,*" *he whispers.*

How such a tiny, one-syllable word can release both a kaleidoscope of butterflies inside me, and a wave of heat to my face at the same time, blows me away. I tuck a curl behind my ear and return his smile. He clears his throat and shakes his head to unscramble his thoughts.

"Stor, what are you doin' here? Shouldn't you be at prom with Josh by now?" Luke asks as he descends the stairs, regaining his normal behavior with each step.

"Josh never showed." My voice shakes, and I clear my throat to steady it. "And I didn't want to waste a perfectly good dress. So, I thought I'd come by and see if you wanna go with me." I bite my lip. "What do you think?" I say spinning slowly to hide my nerves.

The same feeling I had the night I kissed him at Liz's house returns and I punch it down like Ma does with her rising bread dough. Jenna's comments about Luke and me not fitting rush to the front of my thoughts. The fear of being denied fills my chest, and suddenly, I want to run away from him just like before. I can reject myself first so the sting of Luke's 'no' can be avoided.

Not ever telling Luke how I feel about him isn't just because I feel undeserving of him, but also for self-preservation. Never putting myself at risk to lose him, means I'll always get to keep him. Even if it also means I can never love him out in the open. Even if it means I have to watch the captain of the cheer squad take my place in his truck. Even if it means that I'm the only one on Earth (besides Liz) who knows how much I love him.

He smiles again, sending a flood of relief over me, quieting my demons. I'm grateful I took off my heels already, because if I hadn't, I'd fall head over them.

"Yeah. Of course! I'd love to." But then he hesitates. "Uh, I don't have a suit to wear."

Ma interjects. "I'm sure Pa's got something from his youth in the back of our closet. Go grab him and try some things on. I'll keep Story company in the kitchen," Ma says as she grabs my elbow and leads me down the hallway. "Have a seat darlin', he'll be down in a few minutes. Did y'eat yet?"

"No, not yet. We were supposed to go to dinner before the dance," I say, shaking my head.

"Well, I'll make sure Luke feeds you then. In the meantime,

how 'bout you warm up your stomach with a fresh slice of bread? I just pulled the loaves from the oven not too long ago."

"I will never say no to your bread, Ma. Especially if your raspberry jam is included in the deal," I say, as she hands me a slice of her homemade bread. The butter she spreads on it has already started to melt, and my stomach growls in anticipation.

"Of course it is! I make sure to put up extra raspberry jam every year because I know how much you like it," Ma says, handing me the jam jar from the fridge. "Now tell me, who is the stupid boy that stood you up?"

"Well, I wouldn't call him stupid—"

"I would," Ma interrupts. "What kind of boy leaves a girl like you without a date and no explanation? A stupid one, that's who."

"Well, in that case, I guess you'd be right then." I laugh. "His name is Josh, and his parents own the pharmacy on Main Street."

"Oh, I know his family quite well. His folks are nice, but those boys have always been market rats."

A smile steals its way across my face. "No one says market rat anymore, Ma."

"Well, if the description calls for it, I'm going to use it," she replies with a defiant nod. "That boy is not the tea you should be sippin' my dear. He's trouble. And he certainly needs some work on how to treat a lady."

"And who exactly should I be dating, then?"

"My Luke, of course! He's quite the catch."

"Ma ..." I drag out. "How many times do I have to explain to you that Luke doesn't see me as anything but a knobby-kneed tomboy he ran around with as a kid?"

"As many times as it takes for me to convince you otherwise," she says with a mischievous grin.

I'm about to put any ideas she's got to rest when Luke comes down the stairs. He and Pa shuffle into the kitchen and my mind wipes clean. I stand from the table and push my chair in without taking my eyes off Luke. The moment I look at him in that suit I *turn into water. I have no words, no bones, no form. I'm nothing but fluid—unable to move, or speak, or breathe. It's a miracle I'm still upright.*

He holds his hands outward so I can take in Pa's navy-blue suit. Although it fits him a little snug, it's close to perfection. It clings to his wide shoulders and when he turns, my eyes drop to his butt—the suit fits nicely there too. *He finishes spinning and our eyes lock. Neither of us say a word, yet a thousand things are spoken.*

"Well, are you two planning to stand there and stare at each other all night, or are you going to get to the prom?" Pa says, slicing through the moment with his rough, John Wayne voice.

Ma whispers to me, "That was the exact same reaction I had when I saw Pa for the first time wearing that suit." She places my shoes in my hands and gives me a squeeze. "Don't feel bad for staring too long."

Luke and I both laugh uncomfortably.

"Right," I say, clumsily putting my shoes back on.

Luke offers me his arm.

"We've got a dance to get to."

As we leave the house, Ma hollers from the porch, "Don't forget to feed her! She's starvin' Luke!"

Luke gives Ma a thumbs-up. Then he turns to me, placing his warm, calloused hands on my arms. "You look incredible. And Josh is an idiot for missing out on this. His loss, my gain."

"Thanks Lukie," I say, planting a kiss on his cheek before thinking it through. My face flushes, and to hide my already obvious slip-up, I finish with a friendly pat on the back and, "And thanks for being my date last minute."

"I can't think of a better way to spend a Saturday night, I just wish I had a corsage for you." He opens my door and helps me up into his truck.

A few moments later, he comes around to the driver's side holding a single wildflower. He smiles bashfully as he hands it to me and then climbs in.

"Sorry, this is the best I can do."

"It's beautiful."

That night, at home in my room, I press that perfect purple wildflower in my journal and write about the best date I've ever had.

NINETEEN

Luke

E arly Friday morning, my phone buzzed. I pulled my work gloves off and set my post-digger aside to see who was texting. I hadn't heard from Story since I left her at the airport a week ago, and my nerves were itching to connect with her. After the way things ended—although it killed me inside not to contact her—I wanted to see how long she would take to reach out. There was a fine line between being a gentleman by giving her the space she needed, and putting so much space between us she moved on without me. But I also had my pride. If she was determined to do things on her own, I couldn't stop her. So, when I realized the message was from her, I eagerly opened it.

Story: Hey, Lukie.

That was it? That was all she had to say to me? After having the best fake honeymoon of my life—and hopefully hers too—I got two words? That could either be really good, or really bad, and my stomach tied in a knot wondering which it was.

Luke: Hey. How was your first week back to work?

Story: Do you want the honest version, or the sugar-coated one?

> Luke: Always the honest one. We've never sugar-coated anything between us.

Story: I want to say it went well, considering, but it was pretty awful. I can't tell you how many times I mentally went back to the beach in Nassau.

> Luke: Same here. It's been weird to go from spending every day with you, to not talking at all.

Story: It's been really hard for me to not have you to talk to. Can I renege on the 'needing some space' thing?

My chest got all warm and full-feeling, and I had to stop myself from responding too quickly. I staggered like a drunken sailor between being eager and desperate. *I was both.*

> Luke: I was hoping you would. I'm here for you anytime. I've got a listening ear, and a porch swing with your name on it when you wanna come down. I'll pour you a cold Dr. Pepper and we can watch the sun go down.

Story: That sounds so nice. I could use a respite after my week here.

And before I could talk myself out of it, I typed up a message and hit send.

> Luke: How 'bout you come down for the weekend? You can tell me all about it in person.

Story: I'm not sure, it's kinda short notice.
Won't I be impeding on your plans?

> Luke: I would cancel on the Queen of England
> if it meant I could spend time with you
> instead.

Story: The Queen of England is dead.

> Luke: Well, I'd for sure be canceling on her
> then! Ghosts creep me out.

Then she sent one of those emoji things with happy eyes and blushing cheeks. I wasn't sure what that meant. Whoever invented those things should've provided a dictionary. Those three little bubbles popped up like she was typing something else but then disappeared.

When I didn't get a reply from her after a few minutes, I put my phone away and went back to work. Although my body was digging holes for fence posts, my brain was wandering off with thoughts of Story. I got a whole line of post holes dug before I caught up with myself. I should think of her during hard labor more often.

THAT NIGHT, I swore I heard Story's secret knock at the door. I sat up in my chair, paused the show I was watching, and listened again.

Sure enough, that same knock tapped again.

I tossed the remote on the couch next to me and hustled to the front door. When I opened it, my heart exploded in my chest to see her standing there on the porch with a suitcase in her hand. I rubbed my eyes to make sure I wasn't seeing things.

"You came?" was all my brain could come up with to say. *Smooth.*

"Hi. I decided to take you up on your offer. I hope you don't mind. I just really needed to see you."

My heart raced in my chest. I wanted nothing more than to grab the small of her back, pull her into my arms, and kiss her good. But I held back. I wasn't sure how she felt about me, her life, and what plans she had next. It would be presumptuous of me to assume she wanted me. *But man, did I ever want her.*

"Can I come in?"

The raw vulnerability in her voice tore at me. I shook my head to reset my thoughts.

"Of course! I'm sorry, where are my manners?" I took her overnight bag and ushered her inside.

I guided her to the guest room she designed and watched the smile light up her face when I flipped on the lamp.

"You did everything I suggested, down to the curtains and bed linens," she gushed. "It looks even more beautiful than I imagined it would be."

"Well, you're the only woman in the world who could talk me into 'blush pink' walls and flowery curtains."

Pink was pink as far as I was concerned, no need to call it anything else fancy. But the tint she picked out was beautifully subtle, just like her.

She fluffed the pillows and flopped herself onto the bed, staring up at the ceiling. She patted the spot next to her, so I set down her bag and lay down beside her. We had done this routinely in my room at Ma and Pa's, but this time the electricity hummed like a million volts between us. *If I touched her, would it stop my heart?* Even so, I don't think I'd care if it did.

She sighed as her fingertips brushed against mine, and although they didn't shock me to death like I expected, my heart ran off like a wild horse—bucking and kicking. You'd think after so many years of racing hearts and a belly full of butterflies my poor body would've given out. But each time she smiled, or touched me, or, let's face it, kissed me in Nassau, I only wanted her more. I craved a lifetime of excited anticipation. She was turning me into an adrenaline junkie with nothing but her touch, and I welcomed—no, *needed* the rush.

But as we lay there in silence, staring at the ceiling, she began to cry. At first, I didn't notice the quiet tears that fell down her face and into her hair. It wasn't until she sniffled that I realized how bad she was hurting inside. I turned toward her and wiped her cheeks with my thumb.

"Hey," I said softly, "What's goin' on in there?"

Then the floodgates opened.

"I feel like such a failure." She sobbed. "My life is in shambles, my plans for the future are nonexistent, my job is a pressure cooker about to explode, and my fiancé left me for, get this, the boss' daughter!"

"Seriously? That Daffy chick is your boss' daughter?"

She laughed. "Daphne. And yes."

"I don't give two hoots what her name is. She upended your whole world, so she'll always be that weird Looney Tunes duck to me. Does she spit when she says her Ss too?"

Her tears of sorrow turned to tears of laughter, and that was exactly why I made a fool of myself for Story. I would do anything to make her laugh. I didn't care if the whole world thought I was the village idiot. If what I did made her face light up, and that amazing sound come from her mouth, I was fulfilled.

"Look at me," I said, getting serious. "You are not, nor have you ever been, a failure. Even in your deepest, darkest struggles, you come out swingin'. You are a fighter and you always have been. It's just one of the millions of things I love about you. You'll get through this, and I'll be here to lean on while you get your feet under you again, okay?"

She looked at me and wiped her eyes. "It still takes me by surprise to hear you say that you love me."

I sighed. *So much for keeping everything close to the vest until she felt more ready to decide things.* "Well, I do, and I've kept from sayin' it for so long, it wants to fly out of my mouth every time I look at you. I have watched you grow and succeed and stumble and fall. I have seen your weaknesses and your demons, as well as your highlight reel, and I have loved you through all of it. And now, I get to say so.

"I loved you when you drove off in your car to go make somethin' more of yourself, and I love you now, even when you think you've failed at that. You will never stop bein' beautiful and amazin' and kind and good—even when you don't believe that those are qualities you possess. You do. And I see them. I have always seen them."

She leaned over and grabbed a tissue from the nightstand and wiped her eyes. They always got extra bright green when she cried, like a sunset over prairie grass. And I wasn't sure if that was my favorite color in the world or the shade of yellow she wore to our senior prom.

"I will never understand how you can see all that goodness in me."

"And I will never understand why you can't," I said, resting my head against the millions of fancy decorative pillows she picked out.

"I am such a mess," she said, dabbing at her eyes. "My whole life is a mess."

"Nah. You're just in the preppin' stage. Things are muddy and hard. You're tired and worn out from tillin' up the ground, and fertilizin' it for another season. But you're just readyin' for somethin' bigger to come. Soon you'll see the ground dry out a bit, then little sprouts come up, and before you know it, your life will be as healthy and tall as a cornfield in July."

"I wish I had as much faith in me as you do," she whispered.

"Well, you can always borrow mine until yours is strong again."

She leaned into me and her whole body relaxed. I shimmied a blanket from the end of the bed with my foot, slid my arm around her, pulled her close to my chest and let her be. My hands stroked her hair and traced the skin on her arms. Neither of us spoke another word. Nor did we need to. All we needed was to let our souls touch.

When her breaths deepened and she started to twitch a bit, I knew she'd fallen asleep. So, I flipped off the lamp and melted against her in the darkness. Her steady breaths set the pace of my heart like a metronome, and the rhythm of our bodies existing together lulled me into a deep, satisfying sleep.

When the sun came up the next morning, I was relieved to see that holding her in my arms all night wasn't just an incredible dream. I thanked God for her—like I did every day and got up to make coffee.

TWENTY

Story

The sunlight peeking through the curtains woke me from the best sleep I'd had all week. Funny how that happened when I had someone to help unload my worries. I wondered if pillow-talk with Luke would be like that every night. I would come to him with my victories or my failures, and then fall asleep listening to the steady rhythm of his heart.

On the pillow next to me where Luke had been was a note in his familiar handwriting:

> *Hey,*
> *I had to get an early start today with Pa, but come on over to the house when you're awake. Ma still makes her famous biscuits and gravy every Saturday morning, and she'll keep some warm for you. There's coffee in the pot. See you soon.*
> *Luke*

I rubbed my eyes and read the note again. My stomach growled as the thought of Ma's biscuits and gravy pulled me out of bed and into the guest bathroom. I raced to shower, ran a brush through my hair, and threw on my "five-minute-face" of makeup. I pulled my boots on at the door and slung my jacket over my shoulders. Mornings were still a bit crisp, so I filled a Thermos with coffee and walked outside. The cold air revitalized my lungs while I walked down the gravel road to Ma and Pa Dixon's.

I rapped twice on the door before I heard Ma yell, "It's open!" I slipped my boots off on the welcome mat and went inside.

"Oh, Story! I am so glad to see you again! My Luke has talked about you non-stop since he got home from Nassau," she shouted through the doorway in the kitchen.

I smiled. Ma said *Nassau* like *lasso* just like Luke did, and it warmed my heart that his idiosyncrasy had spread. Soon he was going to have the whole town pronouncing it like that, and I didn't mind at all.

The closer I got to the kitchen at the back of Ma and Pa's farmhouse, the stronger the smell of homemade biscuits and gravy hit my nose. I breathed in deeply and smiled as Ma met me in the hallway. There was only one thing in the world that could keep me from devouring Ma's breakfast, and that was the soft, warm hug she wrapped around me.

If Ma's hugs were a comfort food, they'd be fresh-from-the-oven cinnamon rolls with extra gooey cream cheese frosting poured all over. I melted into her arms and sighed.

"You always know exactly what a girl needs."

"Oh, yeah? And what's that, dear?"

"A hug from you and a belly full of your cooking," I said with a grin.

"Well, you got the hug, let's fill you up," she said, stepping away from me to pull my dish from the oven. "I've been keepin' these warm for you since the boys left. I hope they still taste good."

I washed my hands at the kitchen sink and sat eagerly at the table. As the hot plate passed in front of my nose, I inhaled. My mama was a pretty good cook, but her meals paled in comparison to Ma's.

As the first forkful passed my lips, I hummed with satisfaction. "Mmmmmm. They're perfect, like always, Ma. Thanks for saving me some."

"Of course, darlin'. D'ya mind if I sit and do some work at the table while you eat?"

"Not one bit," I replied with another forkful going in. "Whatcha working on?"

"Ah, just balancing the books and the like," she said, turning pages over and typing onto a handheld calculator. She exhaled sharply and forced a smile.

"Ma, I could take a look at these for you. I do that kind of thing for a living. They say I have a knack for finding places where money is hemorrhaging, so if you needed an extra pair of eyes on it, I'd be happy to help."

Ma's eyes lit up at my suggestion. Her and Pa's small farm would be easy to account for after doing giant farms like Hansen Foods.

"Oh, I'd love that! My eyes aren't what they used to be, and I have to do every calculation two or three times just to make sure I did it right. You mess up one year ..."

"I'd be happy to help," I said, finishing my glass of fresh milk and standing from the table. "I'll get my dish washed and run back to Luke's to grab my laptop."

AFTER ABOUT THREE HOURS, the stack of papers were added to my spreadsheets and organized. I closed my laptop and slid her papers into a manila envelope. Then I wrote the month and date on it with a marker and handed it back to her.

"Now, here are your hard copies and receipts. At the beginning of every month, I'll come by and we'll compile everything from the month previous and get you squared away."

Ma clutched the envelope to her chest and smiled at me with tears in her eyes. I felt so much satisfaction in that moment for lending a hand. And it was for something as simple as my day-to-day work. Yet to Ma, it seemed to mean way more.

"Story, how can I ever repay you for this? I know you make big money helping fancy businesses in the city, but I can't pay you what they do," she said, reaching into her large, old-lady purse.

I laughed. "Oh, Ma! Even if you could pay me what they do, I wouldn't let you! Now put your pocketbook away. This is my way of saying thank you," I said, pushing her wallet back down to the table.

"For what?" Ma asked, confused.

"For feeding me the best biscuits and gravy on the planet, and for raising Luke to be so good-hearted. In fact," I said as I put my laptop back into my bag, "I probably owe you a lot more!"

Ma dismissed my statement with a wave of her hand. "Now that's ridiculous."

"I'll tell you what. I'll come by once a month and do your books, and you can feed me your best cooking. Deal?"

Ma squeezed me and patted my back. "You've got yourself a deal. I'll even throw in a jar of raspberry jam to go with it."

Then the strangest thing happened as she pulled backward. A glint of mischief flashed in her eyes as she looked away with a smile. Was this some sort of plan I just got taken for, hook, line, and sinker? Did a little old lady hustle me into coming home every month? I bit back a grin and laughed to myself. *Well played, Ma, well played.*

PA WANDERED in a few minutes after noon and pulled his mud-covered boots off at the door. His weary face was dirty and sweat-stained. But the bright white lines where he had been smiling all day were spared the dust that came from his hard day's work. Even at seventy years old Pa was as strong as an ox and worked like one too.

"Pa," Ma said as he washed his hands at the sink, "Story

offered to look at our books, and she promised to come back and help me balance them every month!"

"Well, that's mighty nice of you, Story. But that's such a long way to travel," Pa said, turning to me.

I shrugged. "Ah, it's worth it if I get some of Ma's home cooking," I said, grinning. "I was also thinking that maybe a few more folks in town here might need my help too. I might as well help as many as I can if I'm making the drive down, right?"

"Well, I always knew you'd amount to greatness," Pa gushed.

My face must've shown my confusion at his statement.

He continued, "Look at you now, helpin' out your community farmers with that beautiful brain of yours. Most folks around here think that you workin' in a fancy building in Chicago means you're successful. I think you're successful when you use what you've got to help your neighbor. I know a few others gettin' up there in age like me who would love your help on their books too. You could even make a whole business out of it down here if you wanted to," he suggested with an undertone of ulterior motive.

Ma and Pa must have scheming together down to an art. I was convinced they'd giggle together over it after I left.

"So, where's Luke? I thought he'd be with you, Pa," I asked, looking around.

"Oh, he's next door helping Ms. Manning with her riding lawnmower. It's on the fritz again. I told him I had an extra spark plug. Would you mind running it over there, Story? I am plumb tuckered out today."

"Sure thing," I said as he handed me a small part from his toolbox under the sink.

Ms. Manning lived a few hundred yards down the road in a little white house with an old rickety gate that slammed as I walked through it. I stepped gingerly up the front stoop and raised my hand to knock on the front door. Through the window over the porch I overheard a conversation shared with hushed voices. I paused, unsure of whether I should skulk away or stay put. But when I heard my name mentioned, the insecure high schooler inside me pulled me back by my ponytail and held me in place.

"Well, Jenna has always been better suited for Luke," Ms. Manning's shrill voice wafted through the window. I had high hopes they'd stay together after graduation. She is much prettier than that pitiful girl who was always following him. Story should never expect to have a man as good as Luke. She may have been his shadow in high school, but I'm betting he was just being nice because of his upbringing. I had never seen a more plain-looking wallflower in all my life! She may have been a late-bloomer, but I still see right through her façade, and she's still the same lost girl that sat alone when Luke wasn't there."

"I agree," a voice I couldn't quite place piped in. "Her makeover is only surface-deep, that's for sure. Besides, Luke and Jenna make so much more sense as a couple. You heard that Story got left at the altar, right? That fiancé of hers was way out of her league! I guess she can't keep her man from the city happy. He ran for the hills at the last second with some ex-girlfriend. Luke deserves a woman of a higher caliber, and that's your Jenna."

My heart began to pound, my breath quickened, and although I didn't think it was possible for my heart to break more than it had, that familiar aching in my chest exploded.

Ms. Manning laughed. "I heard that! We talked about that at the beauty shop for weeks! How embarrassing for her. I hope she doesn't think she can come back down here to steal Luke's heart away. I know one thing's for sure, my Jenna knows how to treat a man. He will be way happier with her. Now if he would stop wasting time and just fall in love with her already! I've been breaking that lawnmower for a year now trying to get them back together."

"You have not!"

"I have. And I have no regrets. If I had it my way, Luke and Jenna would be three babies deep already, and that Story girl would never be seen around here again."

"There's no place for her in Little Creek anymore. She moved away long ago, it's time to stay gone," the second voice said.

When they burst out into a fit of giggles, my heart sank and a surge of tears stung my eyes. *Was that what everyone thought of me?* In one gossipy conversation she aired my biggest insecurities and hung them on the water tower for the whole town to see. I hoped by now people would see that I'd changed, grown up, and I was no longer the girl I used to be, but that clearly wasn't the case. And with a gossipy woman like Ms. Manning saying things like that all over town, it made me wonder who else spoke about me that way. I wanted to channel my inner wallflower, fold up inside myself, and disappear from this town forever. I slunk away from the door and stuck close to the shrubs that led into the backyard, blinking back tears as I walked.

As I rounded the corner, I found Luke leaning over the lawn-mower and Jenna staring at him like he was her next meal. She practically licked her lips as her eyes trailed all over his body making a wave of jealousy return that I hadn't felt in a long time. He stood and leaned closer to her so he could hear something she was saying over the roar of the engine, and she grinned as she threw an arm over his shoulder to repeat it in his ear. He laughed as he wiped his hands on a rag and killed the mower, and she basked in his attention, batting her eyelashes. They looked like the perfect couple that Jenna had always insisted they were. Like wedded bliss on a Saturday morning. While he maintained the yard, she showered him with affection. The only thing missing was the two and a half kids and a golden retriever.

My mind flashed back to the first time I saw Luke and Jenna together in the halls at school.

Senior Year

I run through the halls with a letter flapping in my hand, barely able to conceal my squeals. I finally heard back from the university in Chicago that I applied to, and not only did they accept me, but they offered me a full-ride scholarship. My heart pounds in my chest as the excitement explodes within me, and all I can think about is sharing my awesome news with Luke. But as I round the corner in the hallway, I see Jenna Manning pinning him against his locker. The smile on his face and his hands on her perfect hips make it painfully obvious that he enjoys her closeness. When he says something to make her laugh, I freeze. My classmates swarm me, hustling to their next classes, while I stand there like a statue, unable to move. My eyes fix on the girl who has bullied me relentlessly as she steals my best friend. I can't possibly hurt any more than if she slapped me in the face. Until she kisses him. I let out an audible gasp and dive into the nearest doorway to shield myself from the blow. I clutch my chest to keep my heart from shattering as tears burn tracks down my cheeks. Luke's locker slams shut, and Jenna's laughter grows closer. Any minute they'll find me cowering in front of the driver's ed classroom, and humiliation will be added to my heartbreak. So when a crowd shuffles by, I jump at the chance to blend in with them and disappear.

Once again I stood frozen in place, shattered at what my eyes were seeing. When Luke stood to reach for a tool, she grabbed him by the shirt and kissed him. He immediately pulled away, but the sight of her lips on his knocked the air from my lungs. Standing there exposed in the driveway, the lies enveloped me. *Those old gossiping bitties were right: he'd be happier with her.*

I dragged myself toward Luke, determined to get things over with as quickly as possible, when Jenna looked up from their conversation.

"Hey, Pebbles," she said, reaching for Luke's hand to mark her territory. "What brings you by?"

I wiped the tears that stung my cheeks and marched up to Luke, thrusting the spark plug into his hand. "Here's that spark plug Pa said you needed," I said curtly and walked away.

"Stor, wait a sec! Come back!" Luke called after me, but I pretended not to hear him and started running.

TWENTY-ONE

Story

"This was a mistake. I never should've come back here—especially unannounced. I showed up on his doorstep last night, assuming he had no plans. I never should've done that. I never should've involved Luke in my mess of a life, and I *certainly* shouldn't have taken him on my honeymoon! I'm such a fool," I groaned into my hands on Liz's couch.

"You're not a fool!" she insisted, handing me a glass filled with soda and crushed ice.

I sipped it and smiled. *Dr. Pepper, my favorite.*

"I would've made it a Captain Pepper, but I figured it's too early in the day for you to start drinking," she said with a mischievous look over her own glass.

"You'd be right. But I appreciate the sentiment," I replied, squeezing her hand. "Thanks for giving me a place to run to. My parents are having a huge game day party and I didn't want to interfere with my drama.

"That's what friends are for. Now, tell me every juicy detail."

"Well," I began, thinking back on all the things that have happened to Luke and me since the wedding fiasco. "I thought we were getting somewhere. I'm not ready to jump into another relationship, but Luke has always been my dream. I'd be stupid to pass this up because of timing. When we're together I feel like he cares about me. And I've always cared about him ... Then there was that kiss in Nassau that solidified everything. But today I saw Jenna Manning kiss him and I panicked. It messed with my head, and I can't think straight. Seeing him with someone else made me *crazy*-jealous. Yet, I've had years of insecurities built up that won't fade, as hard as I try to overcome them. I can't expect him to wait around for me while I work out my own stuff, but I don't want to lose my chance with him."

"Boy, that's a lot of baggage," Liz ruminated, stirring her ice with her straw. "I have an idea. Let's go to The Waterin' Hole tonight, and you can see for sure how he feels. And if Jenna's there with him, you can dance with every guy in the room until he's as jealous as you feel right now."

"I don't know, Liz. Maybe I should just go back to Chicago and sulk. I am running out of time to figure out what I'm doing with my life before I have to move out of my apartment. I should be packing anyway."

"Well, how Luke responds to you tonight will give you clarity on whether you should move back here and pursue him, or stay in the city and rebuild your life."

I considered her logic, and although flawed, she was right enough. I was almost convinced I could come back home, start my own accounting business, and help out the people in town. But with Jenna thrown into the mix, I wasn't so sure.

"You know what? I think you're right," I admitted through clenched teeth.

"Well, that's a first," she replied, clinking her glass with mine. "Now let's figure out a game plan for tonight."

———

THE UPBEAT COUNTRY music from the live band met Liz and me in the parking lot of The Waterin' Hole. I dusted off my boots as I stepped through the door, and the flood of a Saturday night in a small town hit me. I inhaled slowly, taking in one of the many things I missed about living in a place where everyone knew each other. It was both cathartic and smothering that the eyes of everyone who knew your mother were watching at all times. But when I walked into the bar that night, and one hundred familiar faces greeted me by name, I instantly felt at home.

"Let's get you that Captain Pepper!" Liz shouted over the guitar solo happening on stage.

I nodded, searching the room for Luke as we strolled to the bar. I hoped he'd be here tonight.

"Stop looking for him, girl! He comes every Saturday night to catch up with his friends. He'll be here," Liz insisted, handing me my drink. "In the meantime, let's find some prospects to dance with."

After a few minutes of perusing the room, I felt a tap on my shoulder.

"Hey, Story, it's great to see you. Are you back for good?" a guy I went to school with said to me over the music.

I couldn't remember his name, and Liz saw the panic in my face.

"How's it going, Shane?" she asked, high-fiving him.

I owed her, big time.

"Which one of you ladies can I dance with first?"

"Story would!" Liz said, shoving me into him, nodding over her shoulder at Luke coming through the door.

"I'd love to, Shane," I said, handing my drink back to Liz.

I had to admit, Shane could push a girl across a dance floor, and my cheeks hurt from smiling at how much fun it was. I never realized how much I missed this part of Little Creek until then.

I caught Luke's eye once while I danced with Shane, and instead of looking away, he raised his eyebrows in surprise. But the tune of the game changed when Jenna walked in with a group of her loud, obnoxious friends. She immediately moved in on Luke, hanging all over him like laundry on the line. My blood boiled.

Instead of going WWE and busting a chair over her head like I wanted to, I turned my attention to another guy in the room.

This is about Luke, not Jenna. I made sure to laugh and smile and soak up every minute of every song, whether I was dancing with a partner or in a crowded line dance. While Luke sat uncomfortably with his new female accessory, I did the best I could to overly enjoy myself in front of his watchful eyes.

When the familiar wail from a steel guitar began to play *Amazed* my eyes locked onto Luke's from across the room. He knew as well as I did the memory and emotion behind that song. So when a random guy came to ask me to dance, I wasn't surprised when Luke interrupted the conversation.

"If you don't mind, I'd like to take this one," Luke said in a low, but commanding voice. "I heard Jenna Manning was looking for a partner though, if you want to try her," Luke said, pointing the guy in her direction.

Luke led me onto the floor and pulled me close. I stiffened as his hand found the small of my back, and although I was glad to finally have his attention, I worried Jenna might make a scene because of it. She was a force to be reckoned with and heaven knew if she was anything like when we were younger, she'd have lots of poisonous things to say. After the emotional hit I'd taken this morning, I wasn't sure my delicate self-esteem would survive anymore of her arrows.

"Where've you been? I've been lookin' for you all day long. Luckily, Ben texted me and told me he saw you come in, or I'd have never thought to look here."

"I went to see Liz. She let me hide out for a bit at her place."

"She told me she hadn't seen you when I messaged her."

"Good." I stared blankly ahead. "Are you sure your date is okay with you dancing with another woman?" I asked snidely. I knew I was being petty, but I couldn't help it.

"Jenna is not my date, first of all. And second of all, what on Earth are you doin', Story?" he asked with frustration in his voice.

"I have no idea what you mean, Luke. I'm just hanging out with Liz."

"And dancin' with every other guy in the whole place. Seriously, what has gotten into you? I thought you came to spend time with me this weekend, and I've barely seen you all day."

"Well, you worked with Pa all morning—which I understand. But then you seemed pretty occupied with Ms. Manning's lawnmower," I insinuated more, but my tone was lost in the music.

Luke grabbed my elbow and pulled me outside to the patio so we could hear each other better. He folded his arms across his chest and glared.

"I'm not sure what you saw today, but I can tell you with a hundred percent surety that it wasn't what you thought it was. Ms. Manning has been loosening the spark plug on that damn lawnmower every Saturday for a year so I'll come over and fix it. It's the same song and dance every week. I even save the spark plug from the week before and just keep swappin' 'em. Jenna hangs all over me while I fix it for the millionth time, then I leave. There is nothin' between me and Jenna—as much as she would like that to be true."

"Well, Ms. Manning seems to think there is, and she had some pretty mean things to say about me today with some lady in her parlor. Then after the display in the backyard, it was hard not to believe her."

"What'd she say?"

"She said that Jenna was better suited for you, and that you'd be happier with her. That I will always be a lonely wallflower, and she didn't want me here trying to steal you. She said that I didn't deserve you. That I couldn't make you happy. And you know what? Maybe she's right. Maybe I don't. After all, I can't seem to keep my man from the city happy, because he ran for the hills at the last minute ..."

My throat tightened so hard I couldn't swallow my emotion. My eyes burned and I blinked furiously, determined to keep my head about me in public. I felt so foolish, I wanted to run and hide. But right about the time my fight or flight kicked in, Luke's arms tightened around me and I dissolved into his chest.

His voice softened, and it reverberated in my ear against him, "Who cares what Ms. Manning thinks of you? She's seventy-five years old and is so miserable in her own life she has to gossip about others to make herself feel better. She never has a good thing to say about anyone, so don't feel special."

"Well, in one catty little conversation, she dredged up every insecurity I've had in the past ten years and then laughed about it with someone as mean as she is. So call me crazy, but it's hard not to take it personally."

"I know those insecurities are real to you, but they are unwarranted. Anyone who loves you would never say or think that stuff about you. The people who do say awful things about you are the ones who never figured out how to build themselves up without tearing down another person first. And you don't need their approval anyway.

"I've lived my whole life tryin' to overcome my own inadequacies when it comes to love, so I'm not one to talk about not needin' others' approval. But it's easier to say it to someone else than to put it into practice, right?" He smiled with a twinge of sadness in his hazel eyes.

"So I guess we're both a bit battered and bruised, aren't we?" I forced a laugh and leaned away from him to wipe my tears.

"Yeah, I suppose so. But it doesn't make us unworthy of love. It just makes us more grateful when we find the good kind."

I melted back into his chest and swayed along with him to the rest of the song.

"You remember the last time we danced to this song?" I asked, losing my resolve.

"I could turn a hundred years old and I'd never forget it," he said, smiling down at me.

Senior Year, Multi-School Dance

THE HUMIDITY HANGS *low in the fairground parking lot, and the rhythmic bass from several types of music thumps in the background. The parking lot is already full of the cars of high school students from all over the district, and even though we are on time, it's hard to find a place to park. We end up way in the back row as several members of our group pull up alongside us. The car doors slam through the night, and one by one we gather near Liz's car to wait for the stragglers to show.*

Luke's truck is the last to arrive, and his new girlfriend, Jenna, looks at me with a smug expression as she climbs out of the passenger seat and shuts the door. I'm still struggling to get used to them as a couple, and I think that shows in the disappointment on my face. It singes the edges of my heart to see her riding shotgun—in my spot. But Luke seems happy, and that's what keeps me from clawing her eyes out.

I reach into Liz's trunk to hide my purse inside. Jenna leans over to me and whispers so only I hear, "I see the way you're looking at Luke, and I want to remind you that he is mine. You are a pebble in my shoe, and if I had it my way, I'd have tossed you out long ago." She laughs. "In fact, that's the perfect nickname for you! Pebbles! That's what I'm going to call you now!" She stands, looking down on me and says quietly with a sneer, "Oh, and just so you remember your place, Luke is the only reason you're here. Nobody else wanted you to come, but he insisted on it.

"You are not one of us, and you never will be. Even Liz being here is questionable, and she's at least on the drill team. You, on the other hand, lucked out that Luke pities you enough to overlook your pathetic existence in our group, and he's too nice to ditch you. You are nothing but an obligation to him now. A pet he lets follow him. Don't ever forget that, Pebbles." She turns and saunters toward Luke and slides her arm through his.

My heart sinks and I blink as quickly as I can to keep my tears at bay. I know I'm not one of the "cool kids," and that most of them see me as a charity case. But having Jenna spew that poison in my direction, then have to pretend like everything is fine for Luke's sake, kills me.

My eyes burn behind my tears, and my heart pounds in my chest. I want to put my cross-country track skills to work and run far, far away. But I'm miles from home and at the mercy of Liz, who drove me.

My tears breach their banks, so I bend down and pretend to tie my shoe until the urge to cry passes.

I hear his soft, familiar voice, "Stor, what are ya doin'?"

"Just tying my shoe. Go on with everyone else. I'll catch up."

"I've never seen anyone tie their cowboy boots before," Luke teases.

I look up at him and he sees the hurt in my eyes, his whole demeanor changes. He waves everyone else on and crouches beside me.

"What's the matter? Why are you fightin' tears?"

I debate on whether to tell him the truth about his lovely girl-friend. She acts completely different around him, and he's unaware of her mean streak. I know he deserves better, but I don't feel like it's my place to shatter his illusion of her. She is, after all, the captain of the cheer squad and the most popular girl in school. But she's a mob boss in lip gloss. If she were to find out I told Luke anything, she'd release her minions on me and make my life even more awful. So I sigh, fake a smile, and lie.

"I'm fine. Just a bit nervous about the crowds," I say, standing up. I avoid eye contact by cleaning the moisture on my glasses with my shirt.

Luke raises one skeptical eyebrow and shakes his head. "You suck at lyin', Astoria Jane."

My shoulders slump. He never uses my real name, much less my middle name too, so I know he means business. "Yeah, I know. But this is something I need to lie about, and I need you to trust me. Okay?"

He wraps his familiar arm around me and squeezes me in a

side hug. "Okay. But I'm not a fan of you keepin' secrets from me."

I nod and swallow hard. He has no idea.

After paying the entrance fee, Luke and I sprint toward the crowds to catch up to our group of friends. We wind through a swarm of swaying bodies so thick, Luke has to hold onto me so we don't get separated. It's a claustrophobic's nightmare as hands and arms flail in our faces. I'm slammed into from all directions, and the fog machines make it almost impossible to see it coming. The heavy crowds overwhelm me and I'm wishing more and more that I had just stayed home and read a book instead. The music pounds in my ears and I doubt anyone can hear the text messages we keep sending, but every couple of minutes Luke sends one anyway. We know the odds are stacked against us, so we do the best we can.

As we squeeze our way through the country music dance area, my favorite song, Amazed *by Lonestar, begins wailing from the speakers. Luke stops abruptly and turns to face me.*

"What are you doing? Why'd you stop?" I shout over the music. "We'll never catch up if we stop!"

"Can't waste your favorite song," he replies with a grin, pulling me closer to him than I have been in years.

My heart leaps into my throat and I inhale slowly to keep my demeanor cool. But all I manage to do is get a subtle whiff of his cologne, which makes my heart stampede. "But what about the rest of our group? What about Jenna? Won't she be mad if her date is dancing with another girl?" I protest weakly.

Luke laughs. "It's just a dance, not a make-out session. And she's probably off flirting with some guy from another school," he says, pressing his hand into my back. "Plus, I'm not too hopeful of our chances of finding them, so we might as well enjoy ourselves, right? Relax and dance with me."

His eyes spark with a fiery mischief and draw me in. I let go of my reservations, wrap my hands around him, and lean in until his cheek rests on my forehead. The words from the song encompass us, but I'm so caught up in having Luke so close to me, I can hardly focus.

My heart races as the lines between friendship and relationship blur. I'm fixated on his body, and how it feels exactly how I imagined it would: strong, warm, safe. I want to stay here forever, memorizing the woodsy way he smells, the way his back moves under my fingertips, and the soothing way he breathes in my ear. Forget the friends we came with, and the fact that in the real world, Luke would never fall for a girl like me. Forget graduation and life after high school. Nothing else matters.

After the song ends, the awkwardness of the feelings between us hang thickly in the air. I peel away from him, and my hand skims down his arm. When I reach his calloused hand, he tightens his fingers around mine and holds my gaze. Luke smiles and his eyes show something I have never seen before.

He studies my face intently, his eyes freely roaming across my features. If this were a romantic comedy, he'd have kissed me, or I'd have kissed him—the moment is that perfect. But Luke is honest and loyal and won't ever cheat. And a guy like Luke has his pick of girls at school. He would never in a million years choose me. I tell myself that every time my feelings for him start to skip down that road a little too far. He'll never love you like you love him, Story. *Still, his hazel eyes light up like fire, making my stomach flip like Jenna and the rest of her squad at the football games.*

Jenna.

His girlfriend. The girl who has all but replaced me in much of his life. The girl who does everything possible to make sure I feel inadequate in Luke's world. She's the one who should be swaying with him under the stars, not me. He has given his heart to her, and I have to respect that. So, before my heart is completely crushed, I clear the cobwebs from my throat and say, "We should probably keep looking for the rest of our group."

As if he snaps back into reality, the flames in his eyes extinguish and he squeezes my hand once before dropping it. "I suppose you're right," *he says, leaning close to my ear, and leads me back through the sea of teenagers to find our friends.*

TWENTY-TWO

Luke

I couldn't lie, having Story here all weekend had been pretty awesome—except for the whole Jenna misunderstanding. I'd been dealing with the nosy women in Little Creek trying to set me up for years. But with Story so close to being mine, I didn't want to entertain the thought of anyone else getting in the way.

I led her out to my truck after we ditched our friends at The Waterin' Hole, and the idea of a quiet night in watching a movie never sounded more appealing.

She fidgeted and hummed under her breath as we drove.

"You okay?" I asked, full well knowing she wasn't.

She forced a smile from the passenger seat and nodded, then paused and shook her head. "Actually, no. I'm not. My mind is racing, and I'm not sure how to sort it all out."

"Pick a topic floatin' past, latch onto it, and throw it out there. We can start wherever you want to."

She opened her mouth like she was going to say something, then changed her mind a few times before she blurted out, "I don't want to be honest with you!"

I laughed. "Honest about what?"

Her hesitation hung in the air like the leather-scented air freshener dangling from the rear-view mirror.

"About how crappy it made me feel to see you with Jenna today. And how jealous I got because I couldn't stand the idea of you with anyone else, but yet I'm so freaked out to do anything about it."

Her words hit me like a dust storm and discombobulated my thoughts. "I'm not sure how to respond to that."

"Well ..." She closed her eyes and winced like she was having a silent argument with herself. Then she opened her eyes again and turned in her seat to face me. "Luke, we have been best friends since we were kids. I don't want to leave a ton of things unspoken and have a long, drawn-out miscommunication that could solve most of our issues if we'd just talk about how we feel. We wasted enough years doing that already. So here goes: I care about you. A lot. I have since junior high when I kissed you at Liz's birthday party. I have tucked you away in a special part of my heart for so long because I never dreamed I could have you. And on top of that, Jenna was always quick to remind me how I should never hope to love you, because you were so far out of my league.

"So I guess I used that as an excuse not to try. That way I wouldn't ruin our friendship if things went sideways. But now here we are, at an age when a future can be realized. You're single, and I'm single, and the only thing keeping us from becoming anything more is ..."

"Is what?" I asked, with more desperation in my voice than I wanted to reveal.

"Well, I'm not sure on your part. But for mine, the only thing I can come up with is fear. Fear of leaving a comfortable life behind. Fear of becoming the subject of the town gossip again. Fear of ruining the relationship we have. Fear of failure—I'm so scared of what comes next that it cripples me when I think about it."

"Well, in the name of being honest, I'm afraid too," I confessed. "I've wanted to marry you since that time you took me to see that possum nest by the creek. I made my mind up right then and there that if I was lucky enough to have you choose me I'd take your hand and leap. Then, the summer I turned thirteen my family came out to visit, remember?"

She nodded.

I continued, "After we dropped you off at your house one night, my dad turned to me and said, 'Son, I know by the way you look at Story you've got your sights set on her. But a girl like that deserves more than life on a farm, strugglin' to make ends meet. A girl like that needs a husband who can give her the world, and that man is not a farm-boy from Nebraska,'" my voice faltered as the pain of my father's words stabbed me in the heart. No matter how much time had passed, it still stung like it did the day he spoke them. "And I've felt unworthy of you ever since."

Her eyes filled with tears. "Like being a farm-boy from Nebraska is something to be ashamed of? That's actually one of my favorite things about you, and I wouldn't change that, or anything else about you, Luke."

I smiled, but I could only muster half of one. I hated feeling inadequate. "All I'm sayin', is you're not the only one who has felt unworthy of real love all these years. But you've got to stop puttin' so much importance on what others think of ya."

"I don't know how not to," she whispered.

"You've always pushed yourself to your limits to prove yourself to everyone else. Don't you think it's time to let that go now? You can just be you, and I guarantee, no one worth their salt will be disappointed in that."

"Well, don't you think it's time to let go of the unworthiness your father instilled in you too?" she countered.

Touché, Story. She had me there.

"You are one of the most selfless and loving people I know. That speaks volumes about the kind of man you are and whose love you 'deserve.' If anything, I'm unworthy of you ... Because what kept me from loving you outwardly all these years is the fact that I'm a coward, and I believed the lies Jenna and her friends told me about me not fitting in."

"Well, we aren't in high school anymore, and the opinions of others shouldn't keep us from bein' happy, right?" I replied.

She shrugged. "I suppose you're right. Looks like we're both guilty of letting what others think rule our hearts."

I pulled into my driveway and killed the engine. "So the question now is are we going to let that continue? Or can we shake off the insecurities and unfair expectations of ourselves and move forward?

"We have two choices: we can go inside and watch *The Princess Bride* for the millionth time. Or we can sort through everything you've got swirlin' around in that pretty lil' head of yours—and this messed-up head of mine. You decide." I hopped out of my side of the truck and circled the front to open her door.

She reached out unsteadily and gripped my shoulders as I helped lower her to the ground. She slid down my body and pulled her feet up just before they hit the cement, her breath tickling my neck below my ear.

She whispered, "I wanna lay in your arms and talk and kiss until the sun comes up, so I don't waste any more time before I have to leave tomorrow."

She might as well have set me on fire and dumped a bucket of ice on me all at once, because I felt the heat spread from my neck to the rest of my body, with a rush of goosebumps chasing right behind. My heart pumped like I'd had fifteen cups of coffee, and I raised one shaky hand to the middle of her back to keep her secure against me. If I could do this every day for the rest of my life I'd die a happy man, that was for sure.

"Yes, ma'am," I left a kiss on her forehead as she lowered her feet to the ground and slid away from me.

TWENTY-THREE

Luke

The sound of Story's laughter reverberated through the house I had secretly built for her. And it gave me so much joy to know that these walls—painted in the colors she chose—would hopefully be filled with her love too. I stood in the kitchen waiting for the microwave to finish popping the popcorn and smiled at her from across the room.

"I still don't get how you didn't realize that those Oreos I sabotaged on April Fool's Day were filled with toothpaste! It didn't taste like the original creme filling at all!" she said, laughing from her curled-up spot on the couch.

"Hey. In my defense, I thought they were a new minty flavor, and I didn't suspect that my best friend in the whole world would do me dirty like that!" I protested.

She burst out laughing again and my heart warmed.

"Well, you got your revenge the year after, that's for sure. But in my opinion, your practical joke was way worse than what I did to you!" she replied, pointing her finger at me.

"Um, did you not remember that Ma came after me with Ipecac and made me throw it all back up? You're not supposed to swallow fluoride! Just ask Poison Control. And I ate like half a tube's worth of toothpaste. Then, to top it all off, I had to barf it all back up! Swappin' your water out for white vinegar is not even close to the same amount of payback!" I said, sitting beside her, stealing part of her blanket and handing her the popcorn bowl.

"But I had just come in from my cross-country run and took a huge swig of it! And to make matters worse, I was in the hallway at school and had to book it clear to the other end to spit it in the drinking fountain! It was cruel, I tell ya!"

"Story Madison, you had every ounce of that comin'. And we both know it."

"Yeah, well, you also put regular cocoa powder in my chocolate milk mix ... Which I'm still trying to recover from. I haven't had DIY chocolate milk since, so I got the brunt of that exchange," she said. "My trust for chocolate milk mix is gone thanks to you."

I sat there and smiled like a fool at her. She had always been my best friend; but being able to look at her through a lover's eyes gave her a whole new light. At that moment, she had never been more beautiful—bare-faced, messy hair, glasses, sweats, and all. I considered myself lucky, because a lot of folks got to see her all dolled up, but she saved her dressing down for a select few. And I was a VIP in that group.

We sat face to face, cross-legged on my couch for hours, reminiscing and laughing, and honestly, it was exactly what our souls needed. We had fallen right back into our groove with each other, and I settled deeply into the idea of it being our future. I could imagine nights just like this one, spending time together after the kids were in bed, growing more laugh-lines near our eyes. It made my whole body sigh with contentment. I had never wanted anything else in life but her, and I was so close to getting it.

I changed the subject. "So, there's always somethin' I wondered about, but I was never satisfied with your answer."

"And what was that?" she asked with a yawn and stretched her legs out across mine.

"Why does Jenna always call you Pebbles? I know it's not because you look like the baby from Flintstones, even though that's the excuse you've given me." I watched her eyes cloud over and her smile fade.

She cleared her throat and avoided eye contact.

"*Storrrr*," I said with a warning in my voice. "Don't you shy away from my question now. Look at my face and be honest."

When her gaze shot back up to mine, her eyes were shiny with tears. She clasped her hands together in her lap and rubbed her knuckles with her thumbs.

"So, the old, 'it's just a cute lil' nickname' excuse won't suffice this time, I'm guessing?" she squeaked out.

"Nope. I want the truth. I know you and Jenna aren't on good enough terms for nicknames."

She forced an uncomfortable laugh. "You're right about that. It was more to remind me of my place than to make me feel like I had one in that group ..." She paused to let the hurt pass through her. "She called me Pebbles because she wanted me to remember I was a pebble in her shoe. An irritation in her life, and an outsider among the popular crowd that you were so naturally a part of."

"She what? Why?" I practically yelled as I struggled to rein in my anger.

"Because I was the word nerd, the math geek, the gangly track runner, and she hated that I was an important part of your life. She made it her mission to remind me often that I was unwelcome. She'd give me snide little remarks under her breath when you weren't listening about how I wasn't good enough for you. And that the only reason why I was in our group of friends was because you insisted on it."

By then her tears had overflowed her eyes and spilled down her cheeks. She got real quiet and cleared her throat again, punctuating the end of her explanation. I shook my head in disbelief.

"So, all this time, you've been bullied by her, and you never said anything to me?"

She nodded.

"Why didn't you say somethin'? You meant more to me than Jenna ever would, and I would've dropped her like a bad habit had I known that she bullied you like that." I could feel my blood beginning to boil and I took a deep breath to quell it.

"Because you seemed so happy with her. And I didn't want to ruin that for you. And because she would've made my life a whole lot worse had I done anything to jeopardize her relationship with you. You know the pull she had with the other girls in school! They would've eaten me alive! I was already teased enough, I didn't want it to get worse."

"So you stayed quiet."

"I had to. But at least that way, I got to spend time with you still. Even if I had to share a lot of it with her," she replied weakly.

I shook my head and put my hand over hers looking her dead in the eyes. "You are my number one priority. You always have been. You always will be. Don't you ever forget that. And the next time Jenna comes over to have me fix that stupid lawnmower, I'm going to tell her as such."

"Please don't make a scene," she begged.

"I make no guarantees, Stor. But I can promise you this: after I'm done talking to her, she will never demean you or make you feel less-than again."

Then I pulled her tightly into my arms and flipped on *The Princess Bride*. Her body relaxed into me and I dreaded the morning when the sun would come up and take her back to the city.

TWENTY-FOUR

Story

Driving away from Luke's the next morning was like running with a piano tied to me. After my and Luke's conversation last night and the drama-filled weekend, I was more emotionally exhausted than I had been when I left Chicago.

I dragged myself to the driveway, and it took every bit of gumption I had to put the car in reverse. The hopeless romantic part of me wanted to call my boss right then and quit so I could run back to Luke's arms. But the logical, accountant side of my brain kept interrupting my heart flutters and reminded me to take things slow. It hadn't been that long since the wedding-that-shall-not-be-named, and I was still healing.

When I pulled into my parents' driveway, my mama was waiting for me on the porch.

"Hey, Mama," I called as I swung my door shut and walked up the pathway.

"Hi, baby girl. I am so glad you could come say goodbye before you left. Sorry we had such big plans this weekend. Had I known you were coming I would've cleared the schedule a bit."

"Oh, that's okay. It was an impromptu visit anyway. I didn't expect you to drop your game day plans for me. Besides, spending some time with Luke was nice."

Mama looked at me sideways—the way she used to when she suspected there was more to the story I was telling.

"Mmmhmm," she replied, crossing her arms and biting back a smile.

"What's that about?"

"It's about nothin'. Now come inside and see your daddy. He's been waiting all day to show you his new golf doodinkus."

In my dad's new man cave (i.e. my old room) he was crouched over a putter, concentrating on some new golf mat contraption he'd won in a raffle at the high school.

Mama whispered like we were on a safari, observing wildlife but trying not to disturb it, "So, if you get the ball into that hole there at the end, it'll spit it right back atcha. But if not, you get a loud buzzing noise like you got the answer wrong on a game show. He's been working on his putting distance all morning. I can't hear that buzzer go off one more time or I'll ..."

My mama's new favorite noise filled the room with an unpleasant sound and made us both jump. It wasn't until I laughed out loud that my daddy realized we were there.

"Hey, pumpkin!" he said with a huge smile and crossed the room to give me one of his standard bear hugs. "Did ya see my new golf mat? It was first prize at the fundraiser raffle!"

My daddy's enthusiasm made my heart warm and I smiled. "It's really cool, Daddy."

"Well, I know you've got to be getting on the road soon, so I made us a quick lunch to eat on the patio," Mama said over her shoulder as she headed toward the kitchen. "I made chicken salad sandwiches, and we've got some leftover chips from the game yesterday. There's also an extra bagged lunch for your drive, so you don't have to stop and eat if you don't want to."

"Thank you, Mama, this looks amazing," I said, sitting down at the patio table.

Mama had barely finished pouring us all some lemonade

when the words she'd been dying to say burst from her mouth, "So, you're here to see Luke, hmm? What's going on there? You two have seemed pretty chummy since you left together on your honeymoon ..." she said with persistent eyes.

"Uh, yeah. He's been great through all this."

Mama gave me a look that said I wasn't done talking and insisted with her eyebrows that I continue.

I cleared my throat. I wasn't quite ready to have this conversation, but, ready or not ... "So, right before the wedding that never happened, I found an old letter Luke had written me telling me he loved me. And I felt all mixed up inside about what to do. But he basically shoved me down the aisle and told me to go through with the wedding. Then, Daphne stood up and Dane ran off with her, leaving me with a head full of confusion—as well as relief—and a broken heart. So, I'm just trying to heal and figure stuff out ..." I trailed off, knowing Mama's next question was right on my heels.

"Well, we could've told you that Luke loved you ten years ago, baby," she said with a laugh. "The question that remains is do you love him back?"

I took a deep breath. I had barely let myself consider the answer to that question in the dark, quiet spaces of my mind, much less out loud, and to anyone besides Luke. My palms began to sweat, and I wiped them on my jeans to give my thoughts some traction before I spoke, "I mean, yeah. I do love Luke. I've loved him since I was thirteen. But I want to be one-hundred percent sure that the reason I choose him now is because I want to spend the rest of my life with him, and not because I'm upset about Dane. So, I'm trying to tread lightly on that ..." I slowed my words to a crawl, hoping my confession was enough to satiate Mama.

Her face was stoic, and her silence, deafening. My stomach knot wound tighter, and suddenly I wasn't very hungry anymore. Mama had always been a huge proponent in me getting out of Little Creek to find greener pastures. Or, rather, no pastures at all, but a big city with skyscrapers and taxi cabs honking.

I took a sip of lemonade to quell the urge to fill the silence with oversharing about Luke and me when I caught my dad's face out of the corner of my eye. Was he smiling behind that red plastic cup?

"Daddy, you've been awfully quiet this whole time."

"Well, pumpkin, I want to see you happy. And if that means I get to have an amazing man like Luke for my son-in-law, then I guess I get to be happy too."

Mama nudged him. "Paul, let's not put the cart before the horse, now. We haven't even heard what Story plans to do with her job in Chicago. Don't go pressuring her to come home if that's not what she wants."

"I just want her to be happy. That's all," he replied and winked in my direction.

Mama sighed and took a drink of her lemonade.

I knew she pushed me to reach my full potential so I'd have a chance to live a grand life outside of Little Creek. But the truth was, I loved my hometown. I always had. Sure, I had big dreams to travel and see life outside of Little Creek, but in the back of my mind, coming back was always on the table. That place raised me, and I loved its rustic charm. In fact, after being away for so many years, my heart had grown to love it even more than I ever expected.

"Mama, don't worry. I'm not even sure what's going to happen with work or with Luke yet. Everything is new, and my heart is so raw and wounded. I won't make any big decisions until I can do so without the emotion steering the wheel. But if I do come home, I need to know you're not going to be disappointed in me."

Mama laughed. "Oh, baby girl, there is no way on Earth I could ever be disappointed in you. I thought you always wanted a life in the big city, so I pushed you toward things that would help get you there. Especially if that meant you could get away from all the kids in town that made you feel less-than. Is that why you are afraid to come back? Because you think you'll be letting me down?"

"Well, partly, yeah. That, and the fear that people in town will put me right back in my old box. I'm not sure everyone will accept me, even after all this time. Some tend to be pretty set in their opinions."

Daddy put his hand over mine. "The truth is, honey, you'll never get *everyone* to accept you. But those who love you will be so happy you moved back, that they won't have any room in their hearts for judgment. And I, for one, would love for my only daughter to be back home again. I've missed our morning runs together."

"I have too, Daddy."

A weight lifted off my shoulders, and I felt the release of hesitation leaving my body. It was amazing what a difference a tiny amount of acceptance made.

I checked my watch. "I'd better go if I'm going to make it back to get a good night's sleep," I said as I stood from the table and hugged them. "Mama, Daddy, thank you for lunch. I have missed you both so much!"

As I drove away from my childhood home, the knot in my stomach loosened. I relaxed knowing the pressure I assumed would always be coming from Mama was merely her hope that I'd accomplish my dreams. Ten years ago, living in Chicago and working for a huge firm *was* my dream. But now, it was time to chase a new dream.

I was still unsure about what came next, but a gravel road into Luke's arms sounded better every day.

BEING ALONE with my thoughts for an eight-hour drive forced me to sort out some insecurities I had worn forever like a favorite pair of jeans. My mind kept wandering back to why I allowed the kids at school to dictate who I was. Did I hold Jenna in such high esteem that her opinion of me mattered more than what I thought of myself? Why did I allow her words to sink so deeply in my heart?

Then of course, there was Dane. He was a variation of Jenna, just a bit older. Not that he bullied me the way she did; but he only accepted the parts of me that fit his expectation, and the rest he criticized me about. I had run away from home to escape the emotional toll that Jenna put on me, only to run into the arms of a man who loved me conditionally. Just like with Jenna, I also made his opinions a priority over my own. I had betrayed myself over and over again until I lost my voice.

Had I ever found my voice to begin with?

The changes I had made about myself *were* only skin deep, just like Ms. Manning's guest had said. *Maybe that's why it hurt so bad to hear.* I had changed my outside enough to prop up my confidence, but my self-esteem remained the same: sad, lost, and unsure of myself. I just looked better on the outside.

That night, after everything stilled, I lay in my bed, staring at the ceiling. Every squeak and creak that my apartment made blared like a bullhorn, and my mind raced. Nothing I did quieted the chaos swirling inside. The chamomile tea I made went cold on my bedside table. The hot shower relaxed my muscles but not the pit in my stomach. And no matter how comfortable my bed felt when I fluffed everything perfectly, I could not rest.

I got up and stumbled in the darkness to the bathroom and flipped on the light. I blinked the brightness away until my eyes adjusted, then stared at my reflection.

"Who are you, Story Madison? What do you want?" I whispered.

I searched the sorrow in my eyes until I saw that girl I used to love: the ten-year-old girl that shared random facts about things and had a zest for adventure. The girl who proudly displayed her math test on the fridge. The girl that didn't know that being ashamed of herself was even a thing. My throat strained as I recalled the hateful words, pranks, and laughter at her expense that slowly whittled away at that confident young girl. I wanted to reach through the mirror and pull her close to me. I wanted to tell her that she was priceless—even if some people didn't see her worth. And to tell her to focus on the goodness in people and to believe in herself. I wanted to tell her to never lose who she was inside, because she was beautiful and amazing and strong.

I gripped the edges of the sink and cried harder than I ever had before. I mourned the loss of my younger self and vowed that I would never betray her again.

"I'm sorry I never stood up for you. But that is changing tonight," I sobbed. "You will never have to feel unimportant or alone again."

I wiped my eyes, dragged myself to my room, and fell into bed like a doll cast aside by a bored child. The mental and emotional exhaustion swallowed me whole and cast me into a dark, heavy sleep.

TWENTY-FIVE

Story

I walked into work the next morning with a purpose in my step. No more forcing down anxiety in the elevator or painting on a smile before the doors opened. I was going to give my boss my two weeks' notice, then wrap up every account I oversaw so I could hand them off to someone else. After work, I would pack as much as I could, as fast as I could, and search for places to live near Little Creek. I had made my choice to go home. To choose Luke. To choose *me*.

I set my laptop bag down on my desk and waltzed to Mr. Wallace's office.

"Astoria! Just the person I wanted to see!" he said with a little more enthusiasm toward me than I expected.

"Oh?" I asked, stepping into the doorway.

"Have a seat. I have great news. The board and I have been so impressed with your work on the Hansen Foods account. You've performed so well this year; we have decided to promote you to Accounting VP. Hansen Foods will still be your account, but on top of that you'll have three teams of accountants and their managers underneath you. This, of course, comes with a significant pay raise for you, and of course, more stock options. How does that sound?"

His praise froze my resolve, halting everything about to come out of my mouth about my resignation. I had craved his accolades, and he was sparse with handing them out, making me turn into a dancing monkey at times to bask in his spotlight. It stroked my ego to hear that he was pleased with me, and I was glad I was sitting, because if I wasn't, I'd have lost all feeling in my legs. *Holy biscuits. I did not see that curve ball coming.* My bad habit of pleasing others rolled in and clouded my judgment.

I cleared the cotton from my throat. "Uh, I'm not sure what to say."

"What's there to say, except yes?" he asked in disbelief.

"Right. I realize this is such a great opportunity, Mr. Wallace, I'm just shocked. I, uh, can I have some time to think about it?"

"I suppose so. Although I am surprised you're not jumping at this chance, Astoria. These kinds of promotions don't come along every day."

"Yes. I'm aware of that. But as you probably know, I've had a lot of hard changes occur in my life lately. I was planning to come in today to give you my two weeks' notice."

"Your what? Why would you do that?"

"Well, my goals and focus have changed a bit, and running into Dane at work—especially when your daughter comes in all the time to see him—is kind of a hard pill to swallow. It makes me dread coming into the office." *Wow, Story, how brutally honest could you get?*

I clamped my mouth shut over my sudden urge to over-explain. I was so uncomfortable in the conversation, I wanted to light myself on fire, then stop, drop, and roll right out of his office, just to get away.

"Well, I have to say that it disappoints me, Astoria. I didn't peg you as someone who would let something that trivial get under your skin."

That trivial? Is he kidding me? My groom left me at the altar in front of three-hundred wedding guests—for *his* daughter none-theless—and I was a disappointment because I didn't want to watch them rub their new relationship in my face every day? *Wow, that's rich.*

I bolstered my courage and remembered the promise I'd made to myself in the mirror.

"I didn't expect you'd understand, sir, nor do I need you to. I just wanted you to know that these changes have made my environment here at work less-than ideal, and I don't particularly like coming to the office. I will give your offer a solid analysis and tell you my decision tomorrow," I replied confidently, then stood and marched out of the room.

I high tailed it straight to Olivia's desk to share what had happened, but her desk was empty, and her computer screen was dark.

Is she not coming in today, or is she just late again? I felt alone and a bit defeated without someone to share my brave moment with, and my breath quickened as I walked back to my desk. I forced in a deep breath, swallowed my emotion, and began setting up my computer for the workday.

All day my focus bounced between choosing Luke and Mr. Wallace's offer. The numbers and spreadsheets blurred and doubled, and although it wasn't even noon yet, my mind was exhausted. I didn't trust myself to make a wise decision without spelling it out, so I pushed aside my laptop and grabbed a sheet of paper. On one half I wrote *Pros* and on the other half *Cons* of taking the promotion.

Pro: More money
Con: Money doesn't mean happiness
Pro: A feeling of achievement
Con: Loneliness
Pro: I'd finally hit my goal of moving up the corporate ladder
Con: Success in work doesn't make me feel as fulfilled as it used to
Con: Missing Luke

Con: Trading love for a job I don't even enjoy that much anymore
Con: Taking the job because it proved to others that I was capable and worthy of something
Con: Betraying my own voice to please someone else

I stared at the list for a few minutes and filled in the rest of the cons list with things I'd be giving up if I stayed in Chicago. On paper, everything made sense. But I wished my mind would get the memo to choose love instead of over-analyzing everything to death.

I sighed and buried my head in my hands. I moaned, "My life is a complete mess."

But as quickly as it crossed my lips, Luke's voice interrupted it in my mind: *Nah. You're just in the preppin' stage.*

My heart warmed and the clouds that had hovered over my thoughts all day cleared. I knew the answer, no matter how much money I was offered to stay. I had plenty of money now, and it wasn't what made me the happiest—that was blatantly clear.

I stood up from my desk, crossed the office and knocked on Mr. Wallace's door frame.

"Hello, Astoria. What can I do for you?"

I stood tall, knowing I needed the higher ground to keep my convictions strong. "Mr. Wallace, I am grateful for your offer, but I will have to decline."

"You what?"

"Please consider this my two weeks' notice."

"Is it the money? Because I can offer you more," he said, scribbling a figure on a notepad and flipping it around for me to see.

It was my salary doubled. *Story, stay strong.* "No, sir, it's not about the pay."

My mind raced back to falling asleep in Luke's arms, and the real, bonafide joy he gave me. He loved me for who I was without the fanfare and performance. He loved that girl I cried to in the mirror, even in the times when I didn't. Who better to teach me how to love that girl again than the boy who always had?

"The truth is, I've had a better offer somewhere else for quite a while. And it's time I took it."

"Who poached you?" he asked angrily.

"You wouldn't know him," I said smiling and turned and left the doorway.

TWENTY-SIX

Luke

The minute my head hit the pillow in my guest room I began to melt into the faded scent Story left behind. I'd never admit to the guys at The Waterin' Hole that I'd been sleeping in a pink room because it made me feel closer to her, but it was the truth. It was the only way I could sleep at night anymore, and after watching her drive away after she surprised me last weekend, I'd been restless and grumpy. Even Pa sent me home early today because he said I had a "sour disposition." Whatever that meant. Ma shoved a plate of cinnamon rolls into my hands on my way out the door, and I came home to brood.

After tasting what life would be like with Story as my wife, I couldn't take coming home to an empty house. It was too quiet and dark and lonely without her. She was the sunrise and the birds singing in my life and I needed her. I always had.

I reached for my phone on the nightstand to send her a message before I tried to sleep. I ached to tell her how much I missed her, how I'd daydreamed about our time in Nassau. I wanted to beg her to choose me.

But I didn't.

Luke: Hey. How was your day?

Those three little dots popped up a few times and disappeared before her reply came in.

Story: Hey! I was just thinking about you.
Remember this?

A photo of our senior prom date flashed on the screen.

Story: I found this while packing the other day,
and I couldn't bear to put it away in a dark
box. It's in a frame on my nightstand now.

Luke: How could I forget it? I carried a small
version of it in my wallet for years. Then one
night after too much drinking, Shane shoved
me into the creek, and everything in my
pockets got ruined. I'm pretty sure I punched
his lights out for that one.

Story: You need a replacement one, STAT.

Luke: Yes please.

Luke: That was the most fun I had ever had at
a school dance.

Story: Me too. Why did we waste so much
time going with other people? We would've
had way more fun just going to all of them
together.

Luke: That's how it should've been, for sure.

Story: Can I be 100% honest?

Luke: Always.

Story: I miss you.

Luke: I miss you too. Can I also be 100% honest?

Story: Of course!

Luke: You can't laugh. Promise?

Story: Ummm... I make no promises.

Luke: I'm sleeping on your pillow in the pink room.

Story: You're what? Why?

Luke: Because the smell of your hair is still on it, and it reminds me of Nassau when I used your shampoo.

Story: I KNEW you used it!

Story: Man, Nassau was fun. Wanna go back?

Luke: Every day. But only if you're coming.

Story: Let's do it. I'm falling asleep. Talk to you tomorrow?

Luke: Looking forward to it. Goodnight, Stor.

Story: Goodnight, Lukie.

I flicked off the lamp and settled in, waiting for sleep to catch up to me, but it evaded me like a scared calf at a rodeo. Maybe that was why Pa said I had a sour disposition; I hadn't slept well since Story left. But instead of getting frustrated, I allowed the thoughts of our time in Nassau to flirt around in my head.

Watching her soak up the sun has been branded into my brain

and was by far my favorite memory—besides the kiss we shared on stage, of course. But then there was swimming with the pigs, listening to her sing happily in the shower, how her hand fit perfectly in mine, and the way her hair smelled ... Then my mind skipped ahead to the future.

I imagined standing on the beach, watching Story walk toward me, just like she had described her "next time wedding" would be. Her soft, dark waves blew around her face in the breeze, with a big tropical flower tucked behind one ear. She had spotted a gauzy dress with a slit up the thigh that would work perfectly for our ceremony, and it draped off her tanned shoulders like it was made specifically for her. My eyes bounced between those tan-lined shoulders and her bare feet and that slit as she waited to walk toward me.

Our eyes met, and she smiled bigger than I'd ever seen before. I was convinced that the beach we were standing on had never seen anything more beautiful. My heart hammered in my chest, and I contemplated asking the witness standing next to me if I could lean against him so I wouldn't faint.

When the minister signaled for her to begin walking down the aisle, she let out the cutest little squeal of excitement and I hoped in that moment that every one of our children turned out just like her. I wanted nothing more from this day than to look into her emerald eyes for the rest of my life and to see those same shimmering gems in the tiny copies of her that we'd make together.

I lay there in the dark, letting my mind wander toward a future I could only dream of, without hesitation, completely unbridled and free. If I could just hold onto the memory it had created, I could survive off it until the real day could come.

I sighed with contentment. Tomorrow would be better than today, because imagining a life with Story turned out to be the perfect cure for a bad mood.

TWENTY-SEVEN

Dane

I wandered past Astoria's office for the hundredth time today, and she was so engrossed in her work, she never even looked up at me. I used to love seeing her gaze flick up from her monitor as I went by, the way she stared at me with those emerald eyes like I was the only man in the world. It fed my ego more than I was proud to admit, and if I'm being completely honest, I miss it. I know I let her go, but sometimes I think about what would have happened if I hadn't left her at the altar that day. It wasn't that I was unhappy. Daphne Wallace was more than enough woman to keep me occupied, and I loved her. But I wondered deep down if she'd ever look at me the way Astoria used to. I had to work for the admiration Daphne gave me, when Astoria freely gave it.

I ended up at my destination and sat down across from Mr. Wallace.

"Dane, thanks for coming in, son. How are things going?"

"Fine, sir. Thank you."

"We have a few minutes until Daphne gets here, then we can discuss what I called you in for," Mr. Wallace said, rearranging the papers on his desk into a folder and then closed it with a thud.

I cleared my throat and tried to loosen the knot in my stom-

166

ach. Mr. Wallace made me nervous as an employee, but as the man dating his daughter, that anxiety took on a whole new level. In fact, I suspected he was the reason Daphne dumped me in the first place. He wanted me as the Director of Finance, and it looked a bit too much like nepotism if I was dating his daughter, I supposed. I wouldn't be surprised if he had paid her to dump me ...

I scratched my five o'clock shadow and shifted in my seat. "Is there something wrong with my dating Daphne? Has HR come to you with employee complaints?"

"No, not quite. I have no qualms with that anymore."

Anymore? I sighed with relief and forced a smile.

Daphne burst into the room with her purse and several shopping bags flinging off her arm. "*Hiiii*, Daddy," she whined with a pout as she handed back his credit card.

"Hi, princess. Did you have fun shopping?"

"Sort of. They were out of my shade of lipstick again at Our Lips Are Sealed, so I had to get this yucky substitute that's not the same ..." she said pointing at her lips.

Mr. Wallace shook his head and smiled in disbelief. "Well, I'm glad you found something else instead. Even if it's not perfect. Have a seat, sweetheart," he said motioning to the empty seat next to me. "I need to talk to you both about something."

She lowered slowly into the brown leather chair, dropping her bags at her feet. "What's wrong, Daddy?"

"Well, Astoria Madison turned in her two weeks' notice yesterday, and I am not happy about it. If we lose her, we lose the Hansen Foods account. They only went with us to begin with because they were so impressed with her, and their contract with us ends next month. Without her to show up and work her magic with Mr. Hansen, we will lose a multi-million-dollar account."

"So, what does that have to do with us, sir?" I asked through a dry throat.

"Her main reason for leaving was because her work environment here is hostile with you two putting your relationship on full display here in the office."

"That's not fair, Daddy," Daphne countered.

"I told you two to keep things platonic here in the office, and now look where we are," he scolded us like we were children.

"Okay, we can tone it down. Sorry, sir," I said without looking up at him.

"You'll have to do far more than that to fix this."

"Like what?"

"Daphne, I need you to keep your office visits to a minimum and stop hanging all over Dane when you come. Don't even talk to him."

Daphne opened her mouth to object, but her father's raised hand made her stop.

"Dane, I need you to convince Astoria to stay ... By whatever means necessary," he said in a hushed tone.

"What are you saying, sir? You want me to pretend to want her back, so she'll stay?"

"If that's what it takes."

"But Daddy ..." Daphne whined.

"It's only temporary, princess. Just long enough to get Hansen Foods to sign a new contract. Then Dane can dump her again and she can move onto whatever company is trying to steal her from us," Mr. Wallace said, patting Daphne's hand on the desk.

"I'm not sure I'm comfortable with— "

"Will being promoted to VP of Finance help with that?" Mr. Wallace pressed.

The walls began to close in around me, and for the first time in my career, I felt uneasy about screwing someone over to get ahead. Astoria did nothing wrong, and guilt flooded over me as I agreed and shook Mr. Wallace's hand.

"As far as Astoria is concerned, you two have broken up. Daphne, if you make a scene here in the office, that'll solidify the rumors. I expect you to put on a good show," he smiled wickedly at us both and put his reading glasses back on. When neither of us moved, his face filled with impatience and shooed us with his hand. "You may go. Go on, get it done."

Daphne shoved her shopping bags back onto her arms and walked numbly out the door and down the hallway. As we passed by my office, I pulled her inside.

"We don't have to do this, Daph. Maybe there's another way. I'll go talk to Hansen Foods myself," I whispered, even though the door was shut.

"Oh, don't be ridiculous, Dane. There's no way you can woo that redneck farmer. You're much too refined for that. We have no choice but to go through with this."

"If I wasn't tied up in knots about this, I'd take that as a compliment," I said, pulling her close to me. I kissed her long and hard until all her shopping bags fell to the floor.

"We can't do any more of that here, remember?" she hissed, pushing me away. "But this may be kind of fun. Pretending we don't want each other, when clearly, we do." She giggled. "So, what if we can't be seen in public for a few weeks? We can rendezvous at your house or go out of town for a weekend getaway. It'll be fun and exciting! We'll get to sneak around just like the couples after filming *The Bachelor* is over." She grinned and squeezed my arm.

The idea did sound fun. Plus, no one said no to Daphne Wallace, so I waved my white flag. "So, how do we go about this?"

"I'll start yelling at you and stomp out of your office. Then you come after me and I'll slap you and storm off!" she said with more enthusiasm than I thought necessary.

"Okay. But you'll still come over tomorrow, right?"

"Of course, baby." She cupped my face in her hands.

Like a crazy switch was flipped she started yelling and carrying on. She scooped up her shopping bags and slammed my office door as she left, causing everyone to look up from their desks. I chased her, and I'd be damned if she didn't slap me so hard in front of everyone in the office that my ears rang and my face burned. *So much for pretending—that was the most real slap I'd ever gotten.*

I stood there in front of everyone with my cheek prickling and my head hung in shame. I didn't have to act that part. I felt horrible for what I was about to do to Astoria. After the pain I'd already caused her, I *was* ashamed of myself for agreeing to this. But I couldn't think about that now. I had a boss to impress, a girlfriend to sneak around with, and the promotion I'd always wanted waiting at the finish line.

I'd done worse to people to get to where I was, but not to people who didn't deserve it. And Astoria definitely didn't deserve this.

LATER THAT AFTERNOON I heard a soft knock. Astoria stood in the doorway with an extra coffee and a sympathetic smile.

"Hey. You okay?" she asked in almost a whisper.

I took the coffee from her, and she stood a few steps from my desk.

"Well, I've been dumped and humiliated in front of a huge group of my peers, which sucks ..." I stopped myself. That was exactly what I did to her. The guilt that took up residence in my gut knotted tighter and I forced a smile.

She nodded knowingly, but what surprised me was that her eyes held sympathy for me—not anger—which made me feel crappier. *Why couldn't she just hate me?* I was betting that after this she would.

"I'm sorry things aren't going well with Daphne. Do you want to talk about it?" she asked, lowering into the chair across from me.

"Not really, but I could use some company and a good distraction."

"I can go get my laptop, and we can go over the Hansen Foods account. I found a few things I wanted to discuss with you before

I left anyway," she said, standing. She left the room and returned a few minutes later hugging her laptop.

"I heard you put in your two weeks. You will leave a hole that will be hard to fill," I said as she got set up.

"Thank you."

"Can I ask where you're going?"

"I'm going home, Dane. I'm going to set up my own accounting business in Little Creek to help the local farmers. After working with Hansen Foods, I realized that success can be found in helping your neighbor just as much as in a multi-million-dollar company."

"That's honorable. I admit I'm kinda bummed you're leaving."

"Why is that?"

"Because we made a good team, and we have a lot of things left unsaid. That bothers me."

"Well, now's your chance. I'm sitting right here, and I don't feel the need to storm out ... yet," she said with a slight smile.

"I miss you sometimes," I admit hurriedly before I chickened out. "And I'm haunted by thoughts of what would've been, had things not happened the way they did."

"You chose Daphne, Dane. That's it. And you have to live with that choice, no matter how things ended up between you two."

"Come on, Astoria. Don't you ever let yourself wonder what might've been?"

"For a moment, maybe. But mostly because it would make coming to the office easier. Not only did I love my job, but I got to see you all day. And I was so mad at you for taking all that away from me." She paused for a moment and a light grew in her eyes. "But now, things are different. I've seen what else is out there. I've seen *who else* is out there. And I think it all happened exactly how it was supposed to."

My heart sank. She'd moved on. Already. Yet, so had I, and I did so even quicker than she did. But that didn't take the edge off the lashing my pride had taken today. How was I supposed to get her to stay when she was already letting go?

My train of thought had left the station in a cloud of steam and barreled down the tracks of what might have been until the tapping of Mr. Wallace's knuckles on my door frame sent everything to a screeching halt.

"I can see you two are working hard today. Keep it up!" he said, shooting a look that spoke a thousand words to me, but Astoria was none-the-wiser. He slunk off back to his office and left me to do his dirty work.

"Hey. How about we go out to dinner tonight, just the two of us? For old time's sake?"

"I don't know if that's such a good idea, Dane," she said with hesitation.

"Drinks then. Let's go down to O'Malley's one more time. Like we used to," I pressed.

She sat up straighter and squared her shoulders. "I can't. I've got a lot of packing to do."

"Come on, Astoria, what's the big deal? It's just drinks with an old friend," I said, and pushed the guilt rising inside way, way down.

"It may not be a big deal to you, but it would be to me. I'm not interested in dredging up a bunch of feelings I've spent the last month overcoming," she replied with determination in her eyes.

I held up my hands in submission. "Okay. You win. But I hoped we could have a conversation alone about what happened. Maybe close a chapter for both of us?"

She sighed, shut her laptop, and collected her things. "No, Dane. That chapter closed the minute you left me at the altar. See you tomorrow." She stood from her chair and left my office.

My chest hurt as I watched her walk away, and that tiny vine of guilt I buried inside wrapped itself tighter in my gut.

TWENTY-EIGHT

Story

I sat in my sweats on the floor of my apartment wrapping fragile items in newspaper. My Bluetooth speaker played my girl-power ballads on low, and I hummed softly as my thoughts drifted from my tasks. I felt a little bad for being so direct with Dane today at work, but I wasn't quite sure why. After all, I needed to set clear boundaries with him while I finished up my last days at work, but I usually had a hard time saying no to him. Although I was having to do it more often, it felt foreign to me to shut him down. But deep inside, I still had things left unsaid with him too.

A knock at the door pulled me out of my thoughts and back to my living room. As I stood to get the door, Dane's voice called out from the other side.

"Astoria, I know you're in there. I can hear Avril Lavigne playing."

I sighed, unlocked the deadbolt, and slid open the chain. "What are you doing here, Dane? I told you I had too much to do."

He held up a bag of takeout from my favorite Chinese restaurant and the smell of fried rice wafted into my nose. My stomach growled and I checked the clock. It was seven fifteen, and I hadn't eaten since lunchtime.

"I know. And that's why I brought your favorites from The Lucky Wok."

He knew I couldn't say no to cashew chicken and the best wontons on the planet. I swung the door open and stepped aside to let him in.

"One hour," I said, shutting the door behind him. "And just so you're aware, this was a cheap shot. I'm starving and you used my vulnerabilities against me."

A cocky grin spread across his face. It always happened when he got his way, and I used to love that about him. Now, not so much.

"Astoria, there is something that has been weighing on my mind lately," Dane said, scooping rice onto the plates I placed on the table.

I relaxed into my chair and tucked my bare feet up underneath me. I inhaled and prepared myself for the uncomfortable conversation I knew was coming.

"And what is that?" I asked, trying to sound as even keeled as I could.

I scraped a hearty portion of chicken onto my plate and stole a wonton from the takeout container.

"Well, first, I wanted to tell you I'm sorry for how things ended with us. You didn't deserve to be left at the altar, and had I known beforehand that Daphne still had feelings for me—"

"You would've dumped me *before* my parents emptied their savings account for a wedding that never happened?" I finished his sentence.

"That sounds bad when you put it like that. I didn't mean for it to come across like that. It came out wrong."

"No, it didn't. The truth rarely comes out wrong," I replied curtly. I could feel the anger rising inside me, and I hated myself for still being affected by him. I didn't want to be under his thumb anymore, and the fact that his words made me feel anything at all was not encouraging. "But the thing is, Dane, you took the coward's way out by not telling me sooner that you were still in love with Daphne."

"But I didn't want to be!" he protested. "I thought she'd moved on, so I was trying to as well."

"Then you shouldn't have asked me to marry you when your heart still belonged to someone else. You lied to me. You made me think you loved me when you didn't."

The hypocrisy of my statement rang in my ears, and I stiffened. Although I'd like to think my situation with Luke was different because I had been trying to move on for years, I knew deep down it was in the same zip code as the circumstances with Daphne. The seriousness of their relationship and timing was the only difference for Dane.

His eyes fell to his clenched hands, and I wasn't sure whether he felt bad for what he did, or if he was trying to come up with something to say to smooth things over.

The urge to admit that I was wrong for agreeing to his proposal, because my heart secretly belonged to Luke, fought at my lips. But before I could speak, he continued.

"I'm sorry, Astoria. I never meant for things to veer so far off course. The truth is, I didn't just come here to bury the hatchet. I came here tonight to ask you to stay."

I scoffed. "You what?"

"I came to convince you not to quit. Don't leave. Stay at Wallace and Chambers. You're great there, and no one can do what you do."

I shook my head, trying to wrap my brain around what I was hearing.

"And I'd like to give us another shot."

The itch to confess that I was wrong vanished in my astonishment.

"Your girlfriend—no, scratch that—your ex-fiancée, *just* broke up with you this afternoon! And you're running to me thinking I'm going to take you back? Unbelievable!" I said with an insulted laugh, stood, and walked toward the door. I opened it hastily and held the knob. "You know what, Dane? I let you in tonight because I thought you needed a friend. And because I also have a huge weakness for The Lucky Wok, which you totally exploited. I gave you the benefit of the doubt because you used to be someone I cared about. And maybe, just maybe, we could get some closure on our relationship. But it turns out you're still the same selfish pig you always have been.

"Leave now, and I don't want to see you anywhere in my vicinity, understand?" I shouted and pointed out the door.

My phone rang. It was Luke. Dane lunged for my phone, swiping it out of my hands. He pressed the "accept" button and turned on the speakerphone.

I reached for the phone and Dane held it just out of reach. I shouted, "Luke, this is kind of a bad time ..."

Dane lowered the phone to his mouth and narrowed his eyes at me. "Astoria, I'm sorry, please give me another chance." An evil grin crawled across his face. He grabbed my arm and pulled me toward him.

Before I could get my bearings, his lips were on mine in a forceful, not-at-all-enjoyable, kiss. I pushed away as hard as I could and wiped my mouth.

"Who is there with you? Is that Dane?" Luke asked with hurt in his voice.

"Yes, but it's not what you think," I scrambled to explain.

"Please just talk to me. We can work this out," Dane begged, handing my phone back to me. The damage had been done.

"Sounds to me like you've got your hands full," Luke said angrily. "I'll let you go."

"Wait, Luke. Don't hang up. I can explain."

"No need. I can connect the dots. You hesitated long enough with me to see if you could work things out with Dane, and it looks like you got your wish. I get it."

"No Luke, that's not it at all!" I reeled, my voice panicky and shrill. "Please don't hang up. Hear me out."

"Goodbye, Story," Luke said and hung up the phone.

Dane laughed like a villain in a superhero movie. He knew exactly what he was doing, and if I wouldn't stay in Chicago for him, he'd ruin my chances of going anywhere else.

"I can't believe you did that!" I yelled in his face. Before I could stop myself, I cocked back and punched him right in the nose.

Dane fell to his knees, his eyes watering, and his nose gushing blood. "I think you broke my nose, Astoria! I could charge you with assault!"

I stood above him and pointed toward the hallway. "Get out, now!" I shouted. "Or I'll give you two black eyes to match it!"

Dane scrambled to his feet and staggered down the hallway to the elevator. I tossed his jacket outside behind him before I slammed the door and locked it tight.

The tears welled in my eyes as I frantically dialed Luke's number.

TWENTY-NINE

Story

I called Luke's phone all night long, but it kept going straight to voicemail. Knowing him, he probably tossed it out into the horse trough to avoid my calls.

My throat tightened and I fought back the urge to cry. Instead, I sent an email to Mr. Wallace, called in sick for Friday, and loaded my car up with boxes.

Before sunrise the next morning, I headed out of the city toward Little Creek. My mind reeled with all the things I wanted to say to Luke—that was if he would even talk to me. Dane screwed everything in my life up, and I fought like crazy to hang onto the remnants.

Around noon I pulled into his driveway, just in time to see him stepping out on his porch. He glanced my way briefly, shook his head, and then walked toward his truck. I scrambled out of my car and ran to him.

"Luke, I need to explain what happened last night. Can you please give me a chance?"

He stopped abruptly. "Did you kiss him?"

I froze. "Well, he kissed me."

"Story, I'm afraid you wasted a long drive and a lot of gas to come all the way down here. I won't be hearin' what you have to say. I'm done with ... whatever this ... is," he said, motioning his hands back and forth between us and scowling.

"Luke, you are my best friend in the whole world. You know me better than anyone else, and you're not even going to give me the benefit of the doubt? Or at least listen to me for five minutes so I can explain? Especially after the same kind of misunderstanding happened with Jenna not too long ago?"

"Did you give *me* the benefit of the doubt?"

I clammed up. *He had me there.* "I know I reacted immaturely. But you're better than me. Will you please just let me explain before you make up your mind? *Please?*"

He leaned against his truck door and folded his arms across his chest. "Okay, you've got five minutes."

"Daphne broke up with Dane, and he asked me to get a drink after work."

Luke rolled his eyes, and I realized I'd have to get straight to the point, or my time would run out before his heart softened.

"I told him no, but then he showed up at my apartment last night with takeout. I let him in because I thought he needed a friend, and I thought it would give me that last bit of closure. I had some things to ask him about, and thought that'd be my last chance."

"And did you talk to him and get this 'closure?'"

"Well, not exactly," I replied.

Luke turned and grabbed the handle of his truck.

"Until I clocked him."

"You what?"

"I clocked him. Right in the nose. Brought him straight to his knees."

The corners of Luke's mouth tugged slightly upward, but he remained frozen in place and skeptical as hell. "You always had a great right hook," he said softly.

"I learned from the best." I reached out to touch his arm.

He pulled away, ripping my heart in two, and I knew it was going to take more than me punching my ex to show Luke I loved him. Tears flooded my eyes as he swung open his door and climbed into his truck.

"Time's up. I'm glad you punched your ex, but I don't see what that has to do with me."

"Luke, wait!"

"Bye, Story," he said with sadness in his eyes and shifted into reverse. "I gotta get back to Pa at the farm."

"Wait!" I shouted through his open window as he started to back up. "I put in my two weeks' notice on Wednesday!"

Luke pumped his brakes and put the truck in park. It was only then that his eyes scanned the back seat of my car and saw it piled high with boxes. His eyes traveled back to mine, and his expression softened. "So, you're quitting your job?"

"Yes."

"Good for you," he said flatly.

"I'm not happy in the city."

"I could've told you that."

"I know. But it took a lot of soul-searching to figure it out for myself."

"Well, I'm glad you finally know what you *don't* want. But I still don't see how I fit into this equation."

"Isn't it obvious?"

"No, Story, it's not. What's obvious is how much I've given to you," his voice rose and strained under his emotion. "What's obvious is how long I've waited for you, and how many times I've had my heart all twisted up and destroyed because you have no idea what you *do* want. You can't try out everything until some-thin' sticks. Not when people who love you are waitin'. So, I hope you figure it out, but I can't wait around anymore. It hurts too much."

He put his truck in reverse again and this time, he didn't stop when I asked him to. He just pulled away down the road and left me standing in his driveway with tears rolling down my cheeks and my torn heart in my hands.

"I want you ..." I whispered as I watched his tail lights disappear.

THIRTY

Luke

My throat tightened around the words I wanted to say to Story—but couldn't figure out how—so like a giant chicken, I ran. She was everything I'd ever wanted, but that day, of all days, I was not expecting to be told by the girl I'd always loved that she wanted me too. I couldn't let those words escape her lips. I couldn't let her choose me over having her dreams. Especially when the guy who could give her everything wanted her back.

I pulled into Pa Dixon's driveway behind my dad's car and sat idling in my truck. Seeing evidence of his arrival here in Little Creek gave me the anxiety I had to escape from at lunchtime. I pretended I needed to go home instead of eating with everyone else to get away from my father. He had already reminded me of my inadequacies simply by being present, and I needed a breather halfway through my day to re-settle my mind. *How sad is that?*

It was not that I didn't love my dad, I did. But he used the wrong kind of words to try and motivate me. Instead of telling me when I grew up, I could do anything, he was the parent who shot down my dreams. When I dreamed of being an astronaut or a baseball player, he'd hit me with the reality that not very many people made it that far. I learned quickly to hold the most important dreams I had close to my heart, where he could never find and shatter them. Except for Story.

I couldn't hide her from him. I couldn't hide the way my eyes memorized her face while she spoke, or the way I smiled every time she walked into a room. Dad noticed the glimmer of hope in my eyes when he visited one summer and was quick to put his spin on why I should lower my expectations. I had always felt deep down that Story deserved more than a simple man like me, and hearing my own father say she was too good for me, confirmed it.

For most of my life, I'd loved a girl I never believed would love me in return. And I left her standing in my driveway, wiping tears that I caused from her face.

I hit my steering wheel and cussed. How could I be so stupid? I threw the gear shift into reverse, put my hand on the headrest of the passenger seat and twisted to see out my rear window. I sped down the road back to my house only to find her car gone. *Had I really just blown the best thing that ever happened to me because I was jealous of her time with Dane?* That, coupled with the fact I had been thinking all day how subpar I was in every way, and it made for one bad mood.

Story knew I didn't mean it, right? Did she leave and go back to Chicago? Was she wallowing at Liz's house or crying on her mama's front porch? Wherever she was, she couldn't have gotten too far away, so I sped around town frantically searching for her car loaded up with boxes. I circled her parents' neighborhood at least a dozen times, passed by Liz's place, and went back to mine; but still no sign of her. She wasn't answering her phone, so I sent her a quick text telling her I wanted to talk, then made the drive back to Ma and Pa's. As I pulled into the gravel driveway, my heart leaped in my throat as I spotted her car parked where mine had been.

I opened the front door, stepped inside, and removed my boots. As I walked down the hallway, I heard my father's voice in the kitchen.

"Well, Story, I know Luke's a great man, thanks to Pa helping to raise him, and I'm extremely proud of who he has become. I always have been. But isn't there more that you wanted to do with your life than live on a farm in Little Creek?"

"You ought to tell him that, sir. He has no idea that you are proud of him, and he has always believed he wasn't good enough for you—or for me. That has kept us apart for all this time.

"And to answer your question, I used to think I wanted more adventure in my life," Story replied. "But after moving away, living in a big city, and traveling the world, I realized nothing else felt quite like home.

"I love your son, Mr. Dixon, and I have since we were kids. I just hate that it took me so long to figure out that with him is where I want to belong," her voice shook like it did when she was trying to put on a brave face and not cry. "And now it's all messed up."

"If I know anything about my son, it's that he's as forgiving as his mother. He has a stubborn streak from me that stretches out a mile long, but he has his mama's golden heart. Give him time to cool down and try talking to him again. I am positive he will hear you. He just needs time to let his hurt settle."

I stood hidden in the hallway, completely shocked by what was taking place. I had rarely heard praise from my father growing up, and to hear it now both bewildered and confused me. All this time he made me feel less-than when he was telling others how proud he was of me.

My heart raced and my mind drew a blank. I was grateful no one knew I was standing there hiding, because no words would've come out of my mouth to explain why. I took a deep breath in and exhaled slowly, trying to sort out the feelings my father had dredged up from the sediment at the bottom of my heart.

I ached for years to be someone he was proud of, and yet he had kept the fact that he was a secret from me all along. I didn't know whether to feel angry at him for constantly moving the goal-posts or happy that after all this time, I finally had his approval.

My father's footsteps grew louder, so I ducked into the bathroom and waited for him to pass. Only he didn't. He stood outside the partially open door and cleared his throat.

"Luke, son, what are you doing, hiding in there?"

I laughed and rubbed my neck. "Uh, I walked in on a conversation that wasn't mine to join, so I tried to make a quick exit."

"How long did you stand in the hallway and listen?" he asked, coming in and shutting the door.

"Long enough," I said, anger replacing the awkwardness of being caught.

"You're upset," my father said with surprise. "Did I say something I shouldn't have?"

I scoffed. "It was more like, you didn't say somethin' you should have for the last twenty-five years."

"I don't understand what you mean."

My heart pounded and my mind raced with all the things I wanted to say—no, shout at him. And I would've, had Story not been right down the hall, unaware I was in the house. I inhaled and forced myself to be calm before I spoke, "My whole life you basically told me I wasn't good enough. That my dreams were too unrealistic, that I was unlikely to accomplish greatness. And the worst part—that I wasn't worthy of a woman like her." My voice trembled under the stress of keeping my emotions steady, "I lived my whole life feelin' insecure about my worth—that I shouldn't love Story because I'd be holdin' her back and keepin' her from her dreams. Yet here I stand, after believin' that for all these years, and hear you singin' my praises to the one woman I have always loved, but never thought I could have. I'm confused and so upset with you," my voice forced its way out of my throat, and I struggled to rein it in. "Why would you do that to me?"

"Son," my father said far more calmly than I felt. "You were the type of kid that was only motivated by the things people told you that you couldn't do. Remember when your cousin told you that you wouldn't last three seconds on that young bull on the ranch? And what'd you do?"

"I rode that stupid thing all summer long until I proved him wrong."

"Exactly. And what about when I told you I didn't think you could hack it on the farm?"

"I moved here with Ma and Pa and worked harder than all the rest," I said quietly.

"I'm sorry I made you believe you weren't good enough," he insisted. "Quite the opposite is true. But I thought that giving you the obstacles of doubt would motivate you to push through them and be the best version of yourself that you could be. If the military has taught me anything, it was to push my men to their limits, then watch them blow past those limits. That was the only way to get them to achieve more than they believed they could. And it looks to me like that's mostly true with you, too, except for Story ..."

"I never felt good enough for her, and every time I tried to tell her how I felt, your voice filled my head with self-doubt. I spent years suppressing the feelings I had for Story because you had me convinced that I wasn't worthy of her." Anger rose in my chest like a volcano ready to explode.

My father's tone changed from steady to humble. "The thing with Story is, I knew right away how special she was, Luke. I knew you'd have to fight hard to win her heart because you'd have a lot of competition. I wanted to challenge you to be the best man you could be, because not only would it be good for *you*, but also because she deserved the best man for the job.

"Loving a woman like Story is like growing a flower in the desert. It takes a strong man to hold a treasure like that with gentle hands. I wanted that for you because I saw how happy you were with her. But I never meant for you to feel inadequate. I didn't realize I was causing you so much harm, and I never meant to hurt you. I'm so sorry, son. I hope you can forgive me."

His eyes welled up with tears, and I had never seen that much emotion on his stern face before. His features softened, and suddenly he wasn't a Navy man anymore—but my father. He transformed into the dad I'd always wanted him to be but had given up on a long time ago.

The fence I built around myself to keep his words at bay started to fall, and although I had hoped for this moment for years, I never actually expected it to come.

He swallowed hard and continued, "I wasn't the best father, and I know I still have a long way to go to make up for my faults, but I'd like to try, if you'll let me."

My angry heart softened in my chest and my fists relaxed. If I had learned anything from Ma and Pa, it was to forgive. And frankly, I was tired of carrying all that hostility and insecurity. So, I took a deep breath and tried my hand at forgiveness—just like Pa taught me.

"Uh, yeah. Sure, Dad. I'd ... like that too," I said with an exhale and extended my hand. He pulled me into a bear hug and patted my back instead. I sighed, feeling the weight of the burdens I carried begin to crumble.

"Thank you, son. Now go get your girl." My father grinned and shoved me into the hallway.

THIRTY-ONE

Luke

I headed down the hallway to the kitchen to find Ma sitting at the table alone.

"Where's Story?" I asked with a panicked voice.

"She left, honey."

"Well, did she say where she was headed?" I pressed, pulling my keys from my pocket.

"Not sure. But you could probably still catch her, she took off toward town—"

Before Ma could finish her sentence, I was running out the door and halfway down the driveway. I peeled out on the gravel road toward town, searching for her. I approached my house and relief flooded over me as her car came into view. She opened the door and turned toward the sound of my truck as she got out. Her red-rimmed eyes avoided mine as I pulled in, and she wiped the mascara smears from her cheeks.

I shut the door to my truck and walked toward her, gingerly approaching like she was a wounded animal.

I spoke softly as I reached her, "You didn't leave."

"I wanted to, but I couldn't bring myself to pull toward the highway."

"I'm glad." I exhaled the pent-up nerves away.

"Why?"

"Because I owe you a very big apology," I said humbly. "I let my ego get in the way of hearin' you, I let my insecurity about Dane take over my logic, and I lost my cool. I freaked out when I thought I was losin' you to the same man twice. I'm sorry," I said with my heart in my hands. "You didn't deserve that."

Her wounded eyes met mine and the sting of my actions spread throughout my body. *I am a real piece of work.*

"There you go with that word, *deserve*," she said with a half-smile. "I thought that word wasn't allowed in love."

"Did I not tell you? There's a clause in there, and it's only allowed if one of us has been a complete jerk," I replied, reaching for her crossed arm, and caressing it. "Now, before I so rudely cut you off, you were sayin' somethin' about puttin' in your two weeks?"

"Yeah." She brushed a strand of hair from her face. "I want to come home, Luke. I am tired of existing in loneliness to be successful. It's not worth it. I want to let go of caring so much about what others think of me and instead be proud of who I am. I want to let go of the stereotypes others labeled me with my whole life and just ... be me! And I want to be okay with who that girl is, nerdy, inadequate, and all.

"I want to be surrounded by people who love me. I want to watch the sun go down over farmland and wake up with the sunrise every morning. I want the cicadas and frogs to sing me to sleep—not horns honking and sirens blaring. I want to pillow-talk with someone who wants the same things as me and to stargaze on a blanket in the backyard. I want to wear my cowgirl boots without being ridiculed and be one hundred percent myself without hesitation ..." She paused. "And I want you, Luke Dixon." Her green eyes lit up with tears of joy and a smile crept across her whole face. "I love you with my whole heart! I have loved you my whole life, and it feels so good to finally tell you! I'm just sorry I didn't say it sooner, but—"

I didn't wait for any more of her explanation. I pulled her into my arms and placed my mouth on hers. She tasted even better than before with a confession of love on her lips, and I wanted to savor it. I kissed her slowly, intentionally, with the patience of a saint at first, brushing my fingertips across her jawline and down her neck. Her body rose to meet mine, pressing me against my truck, and I swear, that was exactly what heaven should feel like or I'm not going. I explored her mouth like a gentleman until her hands on my back traveled downward. Then, I wrapped my arms tightly around her and knocked her socks off.

When we came up for air, I whispered, "Marry me."

"What did you say?" she asked breathlessly as my mouth moved to her neck.

"I said marry me."

"When?"

It sounded more like an exhale than a word, and I bathed in its goodness.

"Right now, tomorrow—whenever. As soon as possible, because I can't go another day without you."

A hum of satisfaction vibrated from her throat to my lips, and I smiled against her neck. "Let's fly out to Nassau," I whispered.

She giggled at the way I said it, and her laugh danced into my ears.

"Just you and me. We'll get married barefoot on the beach and not tell a soul. Then we'll stop in Chicago and grab the rest of your things on our way back home." I moved up her jawline and across her forehead. She closed her eyes and let my lips wander all over her face.

"Home," she said slowly. "I like the sound of that." She ran her fingers around my torso and sent chills racing down my back and arms.

"So, is that a yes?" I asked, kissing her again.

"Mmm-hmm." She smiled. "Absolutely it is."

THIRTY-TWO

Story

Two weeks ago, I put in my two weeks' notice, I told Luke I loved him, and I booked two tickets to the Bahamas without telling anyone but him. Two weeks ago, my whole life changed again, but this time, I finally looked forward to the direction I was headed. I was on a path to what I really wanted, and not on one everyone else expected me to be on. I had never felt more liberated in my life. As I closed my laptop for the last time and turned in my name badge and card key, I wanted to run and skip and squeal.

I smiled the whole way home, not only because I would never look back, but because I had so much to look forward to. Luke was on his way to Chicago with a suitcase full of swimsuits, flip-flops, and the cufflinks Pa wore on his wedding day.

Once home, I tossed my keys into the dish on my hallway table and scurried to my room to pack. I blasted my island playlist and shoved clothes into my suitcase with a grin a mile wide on my face. Swimsuit, check. Toiletries, check. Wedding dress?

I rummaged through my closet, and the only thing that could pass for a wedding dress was the one I wore for my dodged-a-bullet-wedding with Dane. I pulled it down, unzipped the dress bag and ran my fingers across the delicate beading on the bodice. Then I hung it back up and frowned.

"Sorry, dress. You're gorgeous, but very bad luck. I'll be selling you on Ebay. This time, I'm going to get my happily ever after," I said, grabbing my flip-flops from the floor. "I guess I'll have to go a bit more casual."

Luke's voice interrupted my train of thought as he came through the doorway, "You shouldn't leave your door unlocked when you live in a dangerous city," he warned playfully and pressed his chest into my back, wrapping me in his arms.

I relaxed into him and let his warmth emanate through me. "Why? Because some roguish stranger might break in?" I replied with a laugh.

"Exactly. How am I supposed to protect you when you live eight hours away and you leave your door unlocked?"

"Well, I won't be far for much longer, and then I'll be leaving *your* door unlocked."

"I can live with that," he said, kissing the top of my head. "Speaking of which, I found an RV storage place I can park my truck and trailer at while we're gone. We need to get it over there by seven o'clock tonight if we're going to make the redeye to Miami. You all packed?"

"Yep! I just finished up! Although, I don't have a cute dress to wear for the ceremony," I said.

"Ah, I'm sure we can find you something once we get there. We can't possibly be the only people in the world who have eloped to Nassau."

I smiled.

"I say it like that on purpose," he whispered into my hair as he squeezed me tighter. "I like how it makes you laugh."

"It's my favorite thing. Don't ever stop."

"Then don't ever stop laughin' when I say it," he said and kissed the back of my head. "Ready to go?"

I shoved a few more things into my suitcase and sat on it so I could zip it up.

"Yep! Ready when you are!"

Luke grabbed our suitcases, and we headed out the door, giggling and whispering like two kids sneaking out past curfew.

This time, I locked the door.

THE BUMPY FLIGHT to Miami made me nauseous, and the closer we got to the South, the worse it became.

"Ladies and gentlemen," our captain spoke over the intercom, "We are approaching a very dangerous tropical storm that has blown in from the Gulf. Air traffic control in Miami has instructed us to divert or turn around, and I've been given the go-ahead to turn back to Chicago. I'm sorry for the inconvenience, but it looks like we're dodging the weather and headed back to the windy city. A gate agent at O'Hare can help get you re-booked on a new flight once we are on the ground."

He turned on the "fasten seatbelt" light for the hundredth time and we tipped in the air as we made our way back home.

Tears filled my eyes. Luke was fast asleep next to me, and I didn't have the heart to wake him with bad news. I couldn't believe that for the second time, the wedding I had planned on having—albeit only for a few days this time instead of a year of planning—wasn't going to happen. I cried tears of frustration the whole way back to Chicago, and when we began our descent, Luke stirred.

"Did the captain say we are preparin' to land in Chicago?" Luke said, pulling out his earplugs.

"Yeah, he did," I replied, wiping my puffy eyes.

"What happened? Why are we goin' back?"

"There's a huge storm headed toward Florida, and we couldn't land, so we turned around over Tennessee and came back."

Luke's face clouded over momentarily with disappointment,

then he forced a smile and cupped my face so he could wipe my tears with his thumb.

"Hey, it's okay. We can still do this. We may just have to delay for a little while."

I nodded and swallowed the lump in my throat and wrestled with the thought that nagged in the back of my mind: *Maybe I wasn't meant to get married ...*

THIRTY-THREE

Luke

S tory got awfully quiet in my truck on the ride back to her house. The air between us hung thick and heavy, and I wondered if she was having second thoughts about marrying me. I cleared my throat, and summoned every ounce of courage I had to ask the question I wasn't sure I wanted the answer to, "Are you changing your mind about me?"

She looked over at me abruptly. "What? No! Of course not. I'm just ... a bit gun-shy about everything. I've tried twice to get married now, and both times it hasn't worked out," she said softly. "I hate that all the feelings from my last failed attempt are bubbling back up to the surface again."

"That's understandable."

"I thought that if we did a spontaneous, spur-of-the-moment thing, I wouldn't have time to be afraid of another mishap. But even *that* didn't work ... It makes me feel like the universe is against me getting married."

She laughed to try and lighten the mood, but I knew she meant every word.

"Well, I don't care how many tries it takes to get to 'I do,' I'll do it if it means I get to lay my head down on a pillow next to yours each night," I said, taking her hand.

"My bad luck streak doesn't scare you?" she asked, tears starting to fill her eyes.

I laughed. "None of this was your fault, Stor. You have to know that. You can't control the actions of others any more than you can control the weather. Maybe the universe isn't tellin' you you shouldn't get married, but that it wants you to have your barn weddin' dream after all, and nothing else than that will do."

She sighed heavily and I wondered if that meant she was content with my reply, or if she'd overanalyze the whole thing in the shower later to sort things out in her mind.

"Maybe you're right. I just really want to be like Prince Humperdink in *Princess Bride* and say, 'Skip to the end!'" she said with sad laughter. "I don't want to keep getting my hopes up for something that doesn't end up happening. Planning and preparing for our elopement was the only thing that got me through the last two weeks of work."

"I guess it wasn't all for nothin' then," I said with a smile. "It had its own purpose in gettin' you through."

She nodded and a bit of her usual sparkle returned to her eyes. "I guess it did, didn't it? And if we don't elope, we can always use our tickets to go back for our real honeymoon."

"Now you're talkin'," I said, putting a hand on her knee. "We'll just be rearrangin' our timeline a bit. Besides, we've never gone with the natural flow of things anyway."

"What do you mean?"

"Well, I carried you over the threshold when you were plastered drunk at eighteen," I began. "Then, we went on a honeymoon before we even got hitched. I'd say we're destined to do things in the wrong order."

"I never even thought about it like that before," she said, smiling.

And just like that, the bright green glow returned to her tired eyes.

The sun crept up over the skyline as we pulled up to her house. My heavy bones reminded me we'd been up all night circling above the eastern part of the U.S., and Story's big yawn confirmed her weariness too.

"How about we go rest for a bit, then we'll start packin' you up to get you back home."

"Sounds good," she replied with heavy eyes. "We've got a lot to do."

"But first," I said as I killed the engine, "sleep."

THIRTY-FOUR

Luke

Story and I slept all morning and worked all afternoon to pack up the rest of her apartment. We moved box after box to my truck and the trailer I towed up with it. At first, I was sure we'd be able to get everything she had in one trip. But as I neared the top of the steps to her third-floor apartment, another stack of boxes greeted me.

She came out the front door as I began to load up my arms.

"Here, let me take some of these," she said with gratitude in her voice. "You didn't have to do this. I could've hired a moving truck."

I laughed, and it came out strained since I was at least an extra sixty pounds heavier. "I'd never be okay with that." I shifted the weight. "Plus, I got to come hang out with you for three whole days. We haven't spent this much solid time together since our first time in Nassau."

She smiled. "Man, that was a great trip, huh?" She grabbed a box and headed toward the parking lot. "It would sure be nice to be on the beach sipping daiquiris right now instead of hauling boxes."

"Sure, it would be. But this whole thing is just a minor setback. We'll be watchin' the sun sink into the ocean before you know it. Those tickets are already burnin' a hole in my pocket," I said over my stack of boxes.

As we got to the bottom of the staircase, Story froze.

"Dane," she said as he strolled up the sidewalk.

"Hello, Astoria." He forced a smile. He tipped his chin upward at me and said dryly, "Luke."

I returned his greeting with the same disdain on my face, but just nodded. He wasn't good enough for my words.

He leaned in close to Story, and I watched her body language stiffen as he invaded her space.

"Can we talk privately for a moment?" he whispered in her ear.

I set the boxes in my arms down on the trailer and walked over to retrieve the one in Story's arms.

"I'll be over there situatin' stuff if you need me, Stor."

"Thank you, Luke." She blinked rapidly and began playing with that strand of hair she twists when she's nervous.

Dane led her further from where I was working, and although I couldn't hear everything that was being said, Story's facial expressions filled in the gaps. And when he reached out to touch her arm, she pulled away like he'd burned her. *That is a good sign.* But that was when his voice got louder, and although she was a good half-foot shorter than he was, she squared up her shoulders and stood her ground. *That's my Story!* I knew that tough, fearless girl was still in there somewhere. It was good to see her again.

"I said no, Dane. You had your chance, and you blew it. Just because things aren't going great with the boss' daughter doesn't mean that you can come crawling back to me."

Dane looked my way, and although I appeared to be hard at work packing the truck, I tried to hang on every word they discussed. Then his voice got low and his eyes kept wandering in my direction while he spoke. I didn't hear what he said, but Story didn't like it one bit.

"Luke is my best friend in the whole world," she replied loud enough I could hear. "He's the one who walked in when you walked out. He's the one who picked up the pieces you left me in and helped put me back together. You may not think he is much of a man because he doesn't drive an expensive car or work in a fancy office like you. But he is one hundred times the man you'll ever be, because he stood by me when you chose to leave." She turned away from Dane and started toward me.

"I should've never agreed to pretend to want you back to save the Hansen account!" he shouted at her.

His words made my head raise and her jaw drop, and she paused in her steps and pivoted. For a moment, she was speechless. "You mean, you're telling me you pretended to want me back to get me to stay at work?" Her voice trembled with anger, and she clenched her fists at her sides.

"Wallace made me an offer I couldn't refuse if I could get you to stay long enough for Hansen Foods to re-sign a new contract. But now that you're running back home to the cornfields with Farmer Joe here, we will most likely lose the account, and I will lose the promotion to VP."

He confessed his devious deeds so callously that I sat dumbfounded. He was more of a horrible human being than I thought, only ever thinking of himself. Now it was my turn to ball up my fists. I stepped up behind her, full-well knowing she had the potential to take him down where he stood. We would have to keep each other in check for Dane to leave here in one piece.

"But now that you've single-handedly ruined everything, go back to Nebraska. This city was always too hard for a hick like you anyway."

She cocked back her fist, and I grabbed it before she gave him another bloody nose. But the fact that he flinched gave me joy.

"He's not worth it, Stor," I whispered low in her ear. "He's just throwin' a tantrum like a child 'cause he didn't get what he wanted, that's all. Let him take his ball and go home."

Dane looked in my direction and said condescendingly, "It takes a real secure man to let a woman be the breadwinner in the relationship." He laughed like the complete jerk that he was.

It finally hit me. Then I started to laugh along with him; loud and a bit crazy-like.

"What's so funny?" Dane sneered.

My laughter stopped and my face turned to stone. "You're afraid."

Dane scoffed at my accusation. "You've taken one too many bucks off a horse farmer-boy. I am *not* afraid of you."

"Not me. *Her.*" I nodded in her direction.

"You think I'm afraid of Astoria? She's a foot shorter and a hundred pounds lighter than me. I am not afraid of someone so small."

"Sure you are. But not because she can overpower you physically. But because she overpowers you mentally and spiritually. Now I get why you were such an ass to her for so long, and why you forced her to dim her light. You see, a woman like Story makes a good man want to be a better man with nothin' but her presence. *You* never had the intention of becomin' a better man, did you, Dane? So, you had to force her to be less-than. That way you could feel more important."

"You have no idea what you're talking about."

"I know exactly what I'm talkin' about. Because she has been inspirin' me to be a better man since before I *was* one."

I pulled her close to me and kissed the top of her head. "I'm not done yet, but I'll work every day to be a man she can be proud to stand beside. Not behind. Beside."

"Well good luck with that one," he said mockingly.

"Same to you. Good luck with your less-than. You will constantly have to be pushin' Daphne down, because with every crappy thing you do to get ahead, you'll shrink smaller and smaller. No amount of fancy cars and prestigious job titles will ever change that."

A flash of fear appeared in his eyes, and I knew I hit the nail on the head.

"Someday. You'll see," I promised. Then took Story's hand.

"You're pathetic," Dane spat.

"I got the girl, dude. And I'm not stupid enough to let her go. Who's the pathetic one?"

We shoved past him, and I made sure to give him a good ol' fashioned dead-arm with my shoulder. On our way up the stairs I looked back at him. He was standing there like a fool, frowning, and rubbing his arm. I waved before disappearing behind Story into her apartment.

THIRTY-FIVE

Story

Getting situated at Luke's kept me nice and busy as I blended my things—and my life—with his. For the time being, I took over the guest room until we could make things official, and I loved that Luke was traditional that way. I loved a lot of things about him, even more so than I expected. Like the way he hummed while he brushed his teeth and the way he made coffee in the morning. He thought he was being quiet but was far from it. All that banging and clanging in the kitchen got me in the habit of waking up with the sun so we could enjoy coffee together on the porch. My heart was content, and I relished in the fact that I didn't need anyone's approval to feel this way.

One Saturday morning, while Ma and I sat at her kitchen table, the doorbell rang.

"You stay put, Ma, I'll get it," I said, standing.

"Thanks, darlin', although I'm not expecting anyone today." She looked over her shoulder toward the door.

I swung open the front door and the smile I had on my face immediately faded. The joy in my heart sank like lead in my stomach and I cleared my throat to make room for words. "Jenna.

What brings you by?" I asked with as much politeness as I could muster—which wasn't much.

"Oh, hey Pebbles," she said, glancing over my shoulder into the house. "Is Luke here? Grandma's mower is acting up again," she said with a villainous grin.

"He's off running errands for Pa. But he won't be fixing Ms. Manning's lawnmower anymore. You'll have to trick someone else into doing it for you every week." I crossed my arms over my chest and gathered my courage for her response.

"Excuse me? You have no idea what you're talking about."

She came toe-to-toe with me, and the country girl inside me was not about to back down. "Oh, I know exactly what I'm talking about, and Luke is privy to your little game as well. We're not playing anymore."

"You will *not* get in the way of Luke and me. We are destined to be together and already would be if it weren't for you! Now step aside and let someone who deserves him have him! You will never make him as happy as I could, *Pebbles*, and you know it!"

I laughed at the boldness of her accusation and her eyebrows shot up.

"You think this is funny?" she yelled.

"Yeah, I do. Because Luke has always wanted me. *Always*. And nothing you can do will change that."

"Oh, we will see about that," she sneered as Luke's truck pulled into the driveway. She turned toward him and smiled at me over her shoulder. "Watch me."

I leaned against a porch pillar with a grin a mile-wide and watched as she strolled flirtatiously toward Luke. Her voice turned from venom to melted butter as she set her trap to ensnare him. He crossed his arms and scowled at her.

"No, Jenna, I'll not be fixin' anything for you or your gossipy grandmother anymore. You must think I'm pretty stupid to think that I don't recognize when a spark plug has been tampered with. I've played your dumb game long enough, but not anymore. I'm done," he said sharply as he passed her and walked up the steps toward me.

He smiled and wrapped me in his arms and kissed me good on the front porch, right in front of Jenna. She frowned and marched toward us from the driveway, refusing to give up.

"This is not the end, Pebbles! He'll get bored of you and your wallflower ways and come running to me for some excitement in his life. Just you wait," she threatened, pointing her finger at me.

At that moment, I had an epiphany.

I never needed to change myself on the outside to feel accepted and loved. I had tried everything from new makeup and hair, to new outfits and attitude. All that was only surface deep, and no matter what I did to change my appearance, those who teased me for being nerdy would always see me as that nerd. What I needed most, and what Luke had shown me throughout the last few months, was that I needed a change of *heart* to be happy. Not only was that so I could learn to love myself exactly how I was—flaws and all—but also, so I could find peace in forgiving those who hurt me.

I needed to let go of the pain Dane had caused me so I could move forward. But I also needed to unburden myself from the weight of my past. I was no better off because I hung on to those grudges, nor would I feel better if I sought revenge. The only way to avenge that vulnerable, nerdy girl deep inside me was to love her unconditionally and to forgive those who made it harder for me to do so.

I smiled calmly and inhaled, releasing all that anger in my heart. "Jenna, you can try every trick in the book to steal his heart, but you'll never succeed. You're fighting against two decades of friendship that turned into the deepest love ever known. There is nothing you can do to shake it. You can try, but let's be honest—we all know you've already lost. Nothing you say or do will make me doubt his love for me or my importance in his life. I know who I am and where I stand, so calling me names only makes *you* look petty. You have been cruel to me for years, and I can't get back the time I wasted believing that you were right about me ... but I forgive you."

Jenna threw her head back and laughed. "I didn't ask for your forgiveness, nor do I need it."

"Well, I'm tired of carrying the anguish that being mad at you has caused me. I'm not forgiving you because you want me to, I'm forgiving you because I need the peace it brings. I hope you find that same peace someday too," I replied, feeling the weight of Jenna's cruelty lift from my shoulders.

"You're even weirder than I thought you were, Story," she scoffed.

A comment like that would've made me cry six weeks ago, but the healing I'd gone through since Dane left me at the altar made my heart fill with pity toward Jenna, not animosity.

"Jenna, you really should give kindness a try. It works wonders," I said and turned with Luke to go inside.

After the door shut behind me, Luke high-fived me then pulled me close. He kissed the top of my head and whispered, "I am so freakin' proud of you."

His warmth poured over me like Ma's country gravy and I buried my face in his chest. I knew, at last, that I had come home.

"WHERE ARE YOU TAKING ME, Luke Dixon?" I asked with a laugh.

He'd spent the last fifteen minutes driving me around blindfolded—circling town—I was sure of it. But somewhere along the way I got all out of sorts, and the sounds and turns stopped feeling familiar. He killed the engine and opened and shut his door, leaving me in the quiet of his truck.

My door opened and I felt his hands on the knot at the back of my head, making sure the blindfold was still secure. Then, his hand slipped warmly into mine.

"You ready?" he whispered in my ear.

"I'm not sure how to answer, given that I have no idea what we are doing ..." I trailed off.

"Well, I guarantee you'll love it." He led me down a gravel walkway. "I've been plannin' this for over a month."

Rocks rolled and crunched under my boots, and I was grateful that when Luke told me to wear a dress, I had the sense to wear a knee-length one, so I didn't trip on it.

Luke left my side only for a minute, and I stood alone in the darkness of my sight, my other senses taking over the information center in my brain. A few feet in front of me a set of doors creaked open, and the wood groaned along with the hinges. The smell of hay and summertime rushed at me as Luke's arm returned to mine. We walked up a few steps and my boots clomped on the hollow wood platform beneath me.

Luke stooped down beside me and took off my boots and socks, further perplexing me. The more I heard, felt, and smelled, the more confused I became.

"Okay," he said, "I'm going to leave you again for a minute. Wait until I say so before you take the blindfold off."

The sound of his footsteps disappeared from my ears, and I stood there barefoot and alone, clasping my hands in front of my soft cotton dress. I felt vulnerable and nervous until I heard his voice from across whatever room we were in.

"Okay! You can take it off now!"

I struggled with the knot at the back of my head until another set of hands joined mine.

"Let me help you there, pumpkin," my dad's voice said sweetly.

"Daddy?" I asked. "What is going on here?"

He lowered the blindfold from my eyes, and the glow from the twinkling lights above hit my retinas. I stood next to my father in the old red barn on an aisle covered with sand that led to Luke. He stood fighting tears in his Sunday best next to Pastor Federicks, and my breath hitched. Ma and Pa, Luke's folks and sisters, Mama, Liz, and even Olivia were among the crowd, standing next to hay bales along the aisle holding wildflowers in their hands. My heart overflowed like the creek when it rained, and the child inside me threw off her shoes and frolicked in the squishy banks of it. I smiled from ear to ear, and Luke echoed my sentiment from across the room.

An acoustic guitar started up in the corner playing, *Amazed*.

My dad looped my arm around his. "Ready, pumpkin?" he asked with a grin.

"For longer than you know," I whispered in reply. "Let's do it!"

We started slowly toward Luke, the sand he had spread on the barn floor sifting between my toes as I walked. The only thing that kept me from sprinting without restraint down the aisle was the fact that Daddy was there holding my hand. Otherwise, I would've squealed and ran and made a complete fool out of myself.

As we passed each participant, they handed me their flower, and by the time I reached Luke, I had a beautiful wildflower bouquet in my hands.

"How on Earth did you pull this off?" I marveled as my father gave Luke my hand.

"I had a lot of help," Luke whispered. "It's not a beach in Nassau," he said looking down at his own bare feet in the sand, "but I did what I could."

"It's perfect!" I dabbed at my eyes with my fingertips.

Luke pulled a handkerchief out of his suit pocket and handed it to me to use. "I came prepared. This one is clean, I promise."

I bawled like a baby through most of the ceremony. When it was time to recite our vows, although I hadn't written anything down, I knew exactly what I wanted to say.

"Luke," I began with a trembling voice, "You are the most amazing man I have ever met! You have a heart of gold, and I am still trying to understand why you gave it to me, but I'm so grateful you did.

"I will treasure it and treat it with the utmost care, because you have given me the most valuable gift of all. I can't wait to spend every day with you until we are a hundred and five.

"I want to laugh with you, cry with you, raise babies with you, and rock on the porch as the sun sets at night. You are my best friend, my first love, and my first kiss. And I want you to be every "last" as well.

"Your love, your friendship, your presence in my life is the air I breathe. I cannot exist without it, though I have foolishly tried. You believed in me when I didn't believe in myself. You loved me at times when I felt the most unlovable. And you encouraged me to chase my dreams, even if it meant you couldn't follow.

"You have shown me what love was since we were children, and I will spend the rest of my days trying to reciprocate that. Luke Dixon, you are more than my best friend, you are my whole heart, and I will forever love you."

"I love you too," he said, pulling me in for a kiss.

"Hey, now wait a minute," Pastor Fredericks interrupted. "I haven't pronounced you man and wife yet! Let's not jump the line here," he said with a laugh.

"Sorry, sir," Luke said shyly. "I've been waitin' on this moment since I was a boy, and my patience is dwindlin'."

"I promise to make it quick, then," Pastor Fredericks joked. "You have the floor, Luke."

Luke took a long, steady breath and his eyes welled with tears. "I don't know if I'm goin' to be able to talk." His voice cracked. "You are so beautiful, and I'm just so grateful to finally be standin' here with you. All I have ever wanted was you promisin' to love me forever, and now I'm the lucky man who gets to stand by your side every day and kiss your lips every night. I couldn't ask for anything more than this," he said softly. "Yet knowin' you, you'll continue to make my life better and better. You've already turned my house into a home, my loneliness into joy, and my best friend into my true love ... I can't wait to see what you do with my last name." He smiled his imperfectly perfect smile at me and squeezed my hand.

"All right, now before you two get to kissing before you're supposed to again, let's do the rings," Pastor Fredericks said with a grin.

Luke pulled Ma's antique ring from his pocket and slipped it on my hand. Then, he pulled Pa's ring for me to slip onto his finger and whispered to me, "Pa's ring is a loaner because I didn't want to spoil the surprise. Ma says she'd be honored if you'd wear hers forever."

We both wept as we repeated the pastor's words in record time, and when he said the words we'd been anticipating, Luke pulled me close, tipped me backward ever so slightly, and sealed everything with the perfect kiss. I decided at that moment that Luke's kisses started strong, and only got better, giving me one more thing to look forward to with him.

That night after the celebration had slowed and the fanfare grew quiet, I rested in Luke's arms as he slept. The moonlight painted with watercolors across his skin, and my fingertips traced the curvature of his strong chest in the darkness. His heartbeat lulled me into stillness as it thumped against my ear and I molded into his body, wondering how I had gotten so lucky.

The day Dane left me at the altar had changed everything. I had been plucked off of my current path and sent down an unfamiliar road I had always hoped for, but never dreamed I could travel. Yet there I was, in the arms of my best friend, my one constant, my ride-or-die. He was mine, and I was his. *Finally.*

That failed wedding day was humiliating and wonderful and I will thank God for it every day I rise, because that one devastation altered my whole life. But more importantly, it changed *me*. And I will never be the same.

Epilogue

LUKE

Ten Years Later

STORY STOOD on the porch holding our youngest in her arms, watching me come in from the fields. The golden remnants of fading sunlight danced in her long, dark hair as it blew softly in the breeze. I stopped for a moment and memorized the view like I had almost every day before that. She smiled at me, and I'm pretty sure after years of good times and bad, she wasn't privy to my little routine. I had stored away thousands of moments just like this one in my mind over the years, thanking God for each one as I lay down to sleep at night.

I returned her smile as I came up the steps and she removed my hat with her free hand so she could kiss my lips. That was my favorite part of the day: working hard and ending the day with a greeting from the most beautiful woman I had ever seen. I sighed and my shoulders relaxed as I buried myself in her goodness. If this was my last day on Earth, I would die a happy man.

"Supper's hot," she said softly in my ear and released her hold on me.

I held the door for her and stepped into the house behind her. "Mmmmm. It smells delicious," I said contentedly.

She laughed. "You say that every night. Even on days like this when I work and only bring home pizza." She smacked my rear and hung my hat on the hook by the door.

"How *was* work today?" I asked as I washed my hands at the sink.

"It was fine. Hansen Foods is looking for a firm to do their books and they messaged me again. You'd think they'd have forgotten about me after so many years," she said, shaking her head. "They've contacted me a few times since my non-compete agreement expired. I'm just not interested in a job *that* demanding anymore. I know it would help with the finances, but I kinda like my small, help-the-neighbors-a-few-days-a-month gig."

"I support you, no matter what you decide." I took my seat at the table.

"I know you do. But honestly, I've been the workaholic who lived for the job before, and I much prefer the titles of wife and mom. I'm way happier now than when I was making six figures."

She put the baby in his highchair and pulled her hair up out of her face. The twins settled in next to her at the table and dug into their pizza like rabid wolves. "Slow down, boys. I don't want to have to give anyone the Heimlich Maneuver tonight," she said, laughing.

Story spooned sweet potatoes into the baby's mouth, and he blew most of it back onto her with a raspberry. I hid my chuckle under my napkin and handed her the baby wipes. My heart swelled at the sight of the most imperfect, perfect life I had ever dreamed of. I felt unworthy of such love, yet grateful I was chosen for it. She laughed and winked at me as she wiped the last bit of sweet potato from her nose.

"I haven't seen Amelia in a while. Do you know where she is?" she asked.

As if on cue, a freckle-faced girl with a few missing teeth came bounding through the back door in a whirlwind.

"Mama! I made a new friend!" she shouted with a face covered in dirt and joy.

"You did? Where?"

"He was in the pasture next to ours; they moved in last week! His name is Jonas, and he loves frogs and climbing trees, just like me! We made a secret treehouse down by the creek and he's going to meet me there tomorrow after school!" she rattled off with excitement. "We're going to be best friends just like you and Daddy!"

Amelia smiled her jack-o-lantern smile as her eyes bounced between Story and me, then she turned and ran down the hallway to wash up.

"I pray you get that very thing, silly-Millie," I said quietly. My chest filled with gratitude as I looked across the table at my dreams come true.

Story glanced up at me from the bowl of baby food and her emerald eyes sparkled. She shot me a knowing smile, and I wished in that moment I could return to her what she had given me. It was a debt I would never be able to fully repay, but I'd die trying. I had a life I had always dreamed of, and it was all because of the day she barreled into my life at eight years old and changed everything. Then, to top it off, she grew into an amazing, powerful, loving woman. And I was the lucky guy who got to give her my friendship, my heart, my grandmother's ring, and my last name.

The End

Acknowledgments

Thank you to my editors and cover designer who helped me get this book polished and shiny. To my critique group: Ashley, Lane, Janae, & Ashley, your advice and tips on my manuscript helped me level-up and I'm so grateful for you all! Thanks for being my tribe.

To Travis, who willingly reads everything I write: I don't know what I did to deserve a man as amazing as you, but I thank God for you every day. Thank you for supporting my dreams, no matter what they are.

To my four amazing kids: I love you a bushel and a peck.

To my mom: Thank you for reading my *very* rough drafts and loving them anyway. Your encouragement keeps me going when I want to quit. I hope someday I can be the caliber of woman you are.

And last but not least, to you, Beautiful Bookworm: Thank you for taking the time to read my novel. I know that there are five million others that you could've chosen, but man, am I glad you gave this indie author a chance! You will never understand just how much it means to me that someone has loved something I created. Thank you.

Reviews

I value your opinion as much as other potential readers do. Please find my books on major retailers and Goodreads to leave a review. Reviews help indie authors more than you know. Also, I'd love to connect on social media. You can find me on Instagram & Facebook: @authornoelledavenport Visit www.noelledavenportbooks.com for a free novella eBook and the latest book releases.